Books by Selina Rose Fugate

Shift the Darkness

I0570685

Shift the Darkness

ISBN # 978-1-78651-964-1

©Copyright Selina Rose Fugate 2016

Cover Art by Posh Gosh ©Copyright 2016

Interior text design by Claire Siemaszkiewicz

Finch Books

This is a work of fiction. All characters, places and events are from the author's imagination and should not be confused with fact. Any resemblance to persons, living or dead, events or places is purely coincidental.

Published in 2016 by Finch Books, Newland House, The Point, Weaver Road, Lincoln, LN6 3QN, United Kingdom.

Finch Books is a subsidiary of Totally Entwined Group Limited.

The Deep Hollows

SHIFT THE DARKNESS

SELINA ROSE FUGATE

Dedication

For Jayden and Cherish. I love you big bunches.

Chapter One

Rebellion

I staggered, holding on to the top of the car door for support. One of my fake nails broke in half as it snagged on the black foam lining of the door's frame. I slurred a string of curses, rolled my eyes, and smacked at the hand tugging at my shoulder. I was just a little drunk, and more than a little stoned. We'd smoked a bowl only five minutes prior and I felt invincible, even if my nails were not. But Steve was annoying me. It was time to set him straight. I'd gotten what I'd wanted for the night.

"Fuck off, okay? I said no. Maybe I'll have a change of heart tomorrow, but as of right now, I suggest you get reacquainted with your palm." I rolled my eyes and made a suggestive hand motion for emphasis.

The tall, lanky, blue-eyed jock in front of me let go of my shoulder as if it had just burned him. The hand he'd removed hung suspended between us, the fingers flexing for a second and crushing on air before he ran them through his stylishly messy blond hair.

His hands went to his hips, and I almost regretted that I'd never see him naked. Earlier he'd taken me out for a cheap burger, told me I was pretty, and had driven me to a well-known make-out point. In Steve's mind, that should have been enough to get him laid. Instead of letting him rip my clothes off to the sweet sounds of the local high school basketball game blaring from his radio, I'd brushed off his fumbling hands and had at once burst out laughing when he'd whispered lines he'd obviously picked up from

5

a badly written rap song in my ear.

Now, standing in the grass of my front yard, I watched with a smile as he tilted his head to the sky, breathing deeply. I knew what was coming, and I waited for it. Steve didn't miss a beat.

His expressive, handsome face, which had been flushed with desire just thirty minutes before, transformed and he gave me the look that every nerd before graduation feared. His top lip quirked up, his eyes narrowed, and the adorable dimple in his chin seemed to deepen.

"Fine, Wren. Doesn't really matter anyway, because tomorrow everyone will think otherwise. I'll even add a tattoo on your ass when I explain in vivid detail how we—"

Giddy laughter bubbled from my lips, cutting him off. "Go for it, Steve, and I'll tell them about the gay porn mags you keep stuffed under the seat of the Jeep." It was entirely untrue, and the lamest comeback in recent history, but I was too high to goad him anymore. I'd never had any intention of sleeping with him, and had purposefully made him believe otherwise, so his anger was somewhat justified. Still, he was a jerk, and everyone knew it.

A mere three months ago he would have snubbed me in the hallway, but now that school was over I was suddenly his favorite subject. Earlier that week, he'd conveniently jogged by my house, sweat glistening on his rock-hard abs with white shorts slung low. I'd been taking out the trash, and he'd stopped and lifted the heavy, reeking bag from my hand and had insisted that he carry it the remaining two feet to the garbage bin. It had taken him approximately five minutes to get my number and set up a date. He'd told me some lame story about how he'd always had a secret crush on me, but was too shy to approach me. I'd said *awww* in all the right places, pretending to be flattered that he'd lower himself to associate with someone as unpopular as myself, and I'd flipped my hair and giggled when he had told me I had beautiful eyes. His confessions had been crap, and I had known it. Three months prior I had been invisible to his

6

kind. But then again, three months earlier I'd had morals and actual goals. As he stood before me now, I faced my own nasty truth—I'd never liked Steve. His self-assurance had made me want to wound him from the moment I'd shown up on his map as a possible adventure. He was a jerk, but really, I was no better. It was a game to both of us. He wanted to take off my clothes and discard me, and I wanted to take the confident smirk off his face. I wanted him to pick himself apart like the girls I'd seen crying in the school restroom after discovering Steve had given the whole student body a detailed description of their lady-bits after seducing them the night before. Most had been virgins, if you could believe the rumors.

I needed to feed the cruel beast inside me that had been growing at an alarming rate. Even I realized that something wasn't right, that something inside me was changing. I was on the edge, which was understandable with all of the crap I had going on, but on some level I knew that it was more than a coping mechanism. Something was ready to break.

But I also didn't care. I didn't care about anything, really.

I staggered into him, pushing my body against his, smelling weed and the expensive cologne his mother had probably bought for him. I felt his muscles tense for a moment, then he relaxed, letting his hand slip down the small of my back with a little more pressure than he'd used earlier.

"Jeez. I'm sorry, Wren. You know I'd never do that, right? You just look so hot tonight, and I'm, you know, getting strong feelings for you."

I snuggled closer, allowing a slow smile to shape my glossy red lips. "I know, Steve. It must be hard knowing that for all of your popularity, and all of your dad's money, the real world doesn't bow to your every whim. High school is over. You're always going to be a big, stupid jock who will never play professional football and will never, ever find out if I really do have a tattoo on my ass."

I kissed his cheek before my words had registered and

7

stepped back quickly before he had a chance to strangle me.

He thought about hitting me. I could tell, but he settled for spitting in my direction and digging the jacket I'd forgotten out of his shiny new Jeep Cherokee. He threw the jacket on the sodden grass, flipped me the bird, then hopped into his Jeep and peeled away. I stood on my tiptoes and cupped my hands around my mouth, not caring that they were stained with resin from my herbal escapades.

"Hey! Thanks for the smoke!" I yelled loudly, my voice cracking a bit with laughter.

I wasn't sure, but I thought I'd seen his eyes glistening with more than the effects of the weed before he'd hopped into the driver's seat.

I giggled, picked up my jacket, and set to gnawing on my ruined acrylic nail all while humming some nameless tune. I staggered through the muggy mid-August breeze, stepping on the cracks of our sidewalk since I was pretty sure a broken back was the least of my mother's health risks, and made my way to the front of our one-story white farmhouse.

Aunt Maggie was waiting just beyond the threshold. Dark circles stood out below her eyes, her hair was thrown back into a messy bun, and the pink pajamas with little cutesy ducklings on them even managed to look ominous. I would have made a jab if I weren't so damn hungry. I'd have hugged her if I weren't so annoyed, but instead I sauntered by, hanging my wet jacket on the coatrack and yawning dramatically into my hand.

"Thought you were gonna be home three hours ago, Wren. It's two in the morning. Where the hell were you?"

I sighed, flipped my hair, and made my way into the kitchen without giving my angry aunt a second glance. I pulled a freshly washed bowl from the dishwasher and searched for a spoon in one of the kitchen drawers. Reaching up, I flung open an overhead cabinet and pulled down a half-empty box of Cocoa Puffs. I flicked open the box top and shook the cereal out sloppily, causing several of the

8

chocolaty puffs to bounce onto the counter. I shrugged, knowing Aunt Mag would clean it later. I scooped up my load and made my way to the fridge where I toed open the door and grabbed a small jug of milk. I cradled it to my chest, almost dropping my cereal, and somehow managed to twist off the lid. When I poured the white liquid over my late snack only a little dripped into the floor.

"What's that smell, Wren? Pot?"

Damn it. I wasn't in the mood, and Aunt Mag was on me unnervingly closely, her nose wrinkled up in distaste.

"Hormones, Aunt Mag. Hormones and teenage angst." I giggled.

I had no idea where that had come from, and instantly regretted it. Mag's face reddened, and I looked away as I began to march out of the room. Then Aunt Mag did something I never would have expected—she grabbed my wrist, and squeezed hard. My bowl of Cocoa Puffs tumbled from my hands, and I was vaguely aware of milk sloshing onto my skinny jeans. The plastic bowl bounced, coming to rest beside of one of Aunt Mag's pink bunny slippers. Chocolaty liquid trembled from one of the ridiculous slipper's bunny whiskers and I kept my head down, watching it with desperation, wishing I could just tell Aunt Mag to go to hell. I tensed to move, but she made a funny little noise that stopped me. I looked up, and Aunt Mag's throat convulsed as she swallowed loudly. Her hair was coming undone from its bun, and almost completely covered her right eye.

"I didn't want to tell you like this, but I would hate for her to spend her last days around a daughter who stinks of weed and cares more about partying than spending precious time with her sick mother. She's going fast, Wren. The doctor says she has a week, and that's an awfully generous prediction. You may not give a damn about that, but I do. That's your mother, who just so happens to be my only sister. Things are going to change, Wren. Things are going to change fast and you're so far away that I'm

9

not even sure you mind. What's happened to you?" Her voice was becoming shrill, borderline hysterical, and the meaning of her words hit me like a bus.

I yanked my wrist free of Aunt Mag's grasp and shot her a dark look—the same look I'd shamelessly used on my now dying mother when she was healthy and annoying, and had intervened in my social life, forbidding me to stay out past nine with the boys I dated. I poured all of my disgust and anger into that look, aware that if I were a decent person I'd be hugging her instead—but I didn't. The damage was done, and Aunt Mag stepped away as if I'd smacked her. Her shoulders sagged and I turned before the tears threatening to spill onto her cheeks began to roll. I showed her my back, kicked the wet mess of a bowl into the corner of the room, and tried to hide the shaking in my knees with a swift escape.

I made my way to the bathroom, squirted some Visine into my glassy, bloodshot eyes, and wished for the millionth time that it was me instead of my mother lying hooked up to the softly beeping IV in the uncomfortable hospital bed we'd had delivered a month ago.

Aunt Mag was right. Things were going to change. Fast. And I had no desire to watch it happen.

Chapter Two
Bone White

I shut out the sobbing of the woman who'd left her quaint, profitable vintage clothing store to care for her dying sister and made my way into the mild, humid night. I slipped in my earbuds, yanked my iPod from the back of my jeans, and blasted rock music so loudly that it vibrated and tickled my eardrums.

There wasn't another house for at least three miles. Perry County was both rural and beautiful. The Appalachian Mountains loomed on each side of the street, quiet, giant and thriving in between the bare areas that had been stripped for coal and lumber. I sniffed the air, earthy with the tang of the fresh rain, then ran my hands through my hair. I didn't know where I was going. I just knew I couldn't spend another minute in the madhouse my home had become. Hopelessness was contagious, and it lived within the very walls.

My mother had a tumor the size of a kiwi in her brain. Once the only heart surgeon in the area, she now lived on the contents of a fluid-filled plastic bag.

"The best you can do is keep her comfortable. Talk to her. If she has moments of clarity, cherish them," the doctor had told us with a genuine pity that had somehow made it all the more terrible. He'd been a colleague as well as a friend, and he'd seemed to be struggling not to cry as I'd wailed into my hands. The vibrant woman had been diminished into a hollow, blue-lipped sleeping beauty. If my father hadn't abandoned us before I'd even been born, maybe he would be there, holding my hand, lending the strength

11

I fought so hard to pretend I possessed. I swallowed the loneliness, stepped over a frog frantically trying to make its way to the other side of the small highway, and sighed loudly. Whenever Mom passed, I'd be under Aunt Mag's care, but the thought didn't comfort me like it sometimes did when I woke at three a.m. from terrible nightmares of my mother's death. Sometimes the dreams were so vivid I'd wake up screaming, and for a moment I'd be sure that they were my reality.

Mom hadn't woken up at all within the last three days, but when she'd woken before, her soft gray eyes had bulged and she'd grasped at the tubes jutting from her nose and the needles in her arms with those once talented, lifesaving hands in a blind, animal panic. Other times, she'd cry, or smile, or do both. She would question me about my schooling as if I hadn't graduated and was back in fifth grade, and I'd nod and play along. Before she'd finally fallen into the deep sleep that cradled her now, sometimes she would wake to clarity, hugging me, telling me it would all be okay, even though she was the one who needed comforting most of all.

"Don't be scared, baby," she'd murmur into my hair, and I'd know that it was all her. She was there with me, alive and alert. And for just a few minutes I would almost let myself pretend that she really wasn't dying. I'd hold her hand like it was a life raft, only to stomp away in tears when she started rambling nonsense or fell back into her coma-like sleep.

As long as I had a joint hidden under the mattress, I could make it another day without succumbing to the grief that threatened to leave me just as lifeless as she was.

But now she was failing fast, and I couldn't stick around to watch her breathing finally come to a hitching stop. In my cold selfishness, I planned on leaving that to my Aunt Mag. After all, she was the adult. She could handle it, right? I felt a stab of guilt, but like every other emotion, I shook it off like raindrops on a slicker and picked up my pace.

My sneakers made wet slapping noises on the pavement, and the dying rain sprinkled my cheeks. It would have been refreshing if I hadn't felt the urge to go drown myself in the pond down the street. The nearest home wasn't for three miles, and therein resided one of the biggest bitches on God's green, mean earth—Chelsea Tanner. She'd spared me her torture for the last year, but I'd never forgiven her for dumping her yogurt on my head freshman year. I toyed with the idea of going back home long enough to snatch a carton of eggs out of the fridge so I could egg Chelsea's Mustang. That might possibly have made me feel a bit better, but I didn't want to risk another confrontation with Aunt Mag. I didn't want to feel the pull that always led me to Mom's room, a small part of me hopeful that she'd be awake, only to be disappointed.

I stopped musing, chewed at the inside of my jaw and stared at the looming mountains on either side. I liked the county. I liked Perry County and our tiny, bustling city of Hazard. I appreciated the quiet, but at that moment I needed a distraction. I needed to be inside a fast car. Even better, I'd like to be the object of a random cute guy's affection. If I could hitch into town, I could likely score a joint. I had ten bucks in my pocket—that would be enough to kill a few brain cells. I stuck out my thumb and kicked at a rock. Silence. It would be a while before anyone drove through, and even then, with my luck they'd know my mother and the only ride they'd be giving me was a ride back home.

Home. It didn't feel much like home anymore. We'd lived in the twelve-room farmhouse for seven years. She could have bought something bigger, something newer, but Mom had fallen in love with the rustic charm and the little barn out back. She was a country girl to the core, and had never considered leaving Perry County in search of a better salary or bigger malls. We weren't rich, but we lived pretty comfortably. The old oak floors creaked with almost every step, and the ceiling sprang a new leak with every storm, but she'd never complained. She was a do-it-yourself type,

13

and had seemed to take satisfaction in making small home repairs.

She'd deemed the barn too empty, and though her busy life wouldn't allow her to have the hearty farm of her dreams, in the spirit of a true mountain woman, she'd bought a goat. Yes, a damn goat.

I'd named him Frogger, because, much to my disgust, on his first night with us he'd eaten a dead frog he'd found on the lawn. Frogger had the barn to himself all night, but early in the morning Mom had slipped out in her slacks, car keys in hand, and let Frogger out to chomp on whatever weird thing he could find. He'd bounce and rub his rough, horned head on her legs and she had spoken to him in cooing gibberish like he was a cute Dalmatian puppy. *'You's a good boy, yeah? Who's duh good boy?'*

Frogger liked to catch me unaware and headbutt me right in the ass. I was the perfect height, and whenever he was out I'd have to watch my back constantly. Love taps, Mom had called them, but I called it terrorism. Now Frogger spent most of his time in the barn, and though he was well taken care of, my aunt didn't have the soft spot for him that my mother had possessed. Aunt Mag planned to sell him eventually at a livestock auction, and really, that was fine with me. It wasn't like Mom would ever have the chance to miss him.

I picked up the pace, then I felt it—someone watching. The fine hairs on the back of my neck stood at attention and a chill sucked at my lower spine. I could have run back home. I was eighteen, healthy, and had never smoked until recently. I slowed my step a little without being too obvious, digging into my pocket to pull out a hair tie. I lifted my hands, trying to keep them steady, and reached to put my thick, long chestnut waves into a sloppy bun. I took the chance to look around, trying hard to appear casual. I picked a soggy, half broken cigarette from my jacket pocket and popped it between my lips. I lit up and kept walking. I wasn't running back home. I was spooked by the darkness, that was all. We lived out in the middle of God's county, and lots of creatures did too. It was probably a deer, maybe even one of the elk they'd been integrating into our mountains for the last few years. Hell, it might have even been a wild rabbit.

My breathing sped up, my footfalls sounding extremely loud in the pregnant silence, and I felt the first spike of panic skitter over my back. I couldn't hear my stalker, I couldn't see the thing that followed but it might as well have been a loud, roaring monster crashing through trees as it ran on clopping cloven hooves. My aquamarine eyes widened, the cigarette dropped from my mouth, and cowardice won. I spun on my heel and bolted for the now-distant light of the farmhouse. I sprinted, huffing and ripping the buds from my ears, tossing them somewhere behind me. I dared a glance back, almost tripping on a stray rock in the road, and my heart squeezed in my chest.

It wasn't a bunny, that was for sure. A man was covering the distance easily, and even in the shadows I could see he ran with the grace of a jungle cat. And that wasn't the only thing that struck me as strangely feline — his eyes were glowing, actually glowing. Red orbs stood out as if he were lit from within like a Halloween pumpkin. I screamed, quickly turning back around before my feet plowed into another stray object. I knew there was a slim chance that Aunt Mag would hear my cry, as the night was quiet and the lack of traffic kept my being heard at least a possibility. I opened my mouth to let out another girly, slasher film chick scream, but it never came out.

I was knocked roughly to the pavement by what felt like a pickup hitting my body from behind. I felt the flesh scrape from my knees and my palms flew out instinctively to break my fall. Gravel bit into the heels of my hands, and I barely avoided my face acquiring some as well. Then I was rolled over and was staring into the face of what I was certain had to be the product of some bad weed. Those burning eyes stared from a clear, porcelain face. His features shone in the moonlight, perfect and terrible. Blond hair tickled my nose, silken and damp with the elements. I bucked, tried to wiggle my way free, but he'd somehow gotten both of my wrists and held them each with one big, cold hand. He smiled, and fangs sprouted before my eyes, thin and dimpling his lower lip.

My best guess was that I was on a bad trip, and the stress from home had sent me into one final nervous breakdown. I tried to squeeze my eyes shut, willing the vision to go away, but they stayed glued open, wide and terrified. I tried desperately to suck back the breath that had been knocked out during my fall, opened my mouth to scream again, but then he spoke.

"Shush."

Then something happened. I felt my body go slack, my fingers uncurl, and I slumped against the pavement. I felt like a puppy rolling over as I settled onto the road, belly exposed, submissive. Distantly I still wished for a random passer-by to come barreling down the road and spot us. Maybe they'd wear a trucker's hat and have a shotgun hanging in the back window.

I was lost in his eyes, my will weakening with each passing, precious second. My tongue no longer worked, and I no longer cared. *This is it*, a calm, sad voice in my mind huffed. And the worst? I never got to say goodbye to my mom, who could be taking her own dying breaths with me in the farmhouse down the street. Not that it was likely she could have heard my farewell anyway, because according to the doctors she wasn't even a person anymore, just a shell. And that's what I was becoming as I listened to the man mumble to himself in another language and stroke my cheek with the back of his cold hand—a shell. I was leaking out quickly. I was broken, and no one would put me back together like they did in fairy tales. The certainty of my fast-approaching death filled me with terror, but it also brought a strange comfort. I wouldn't have to hurt anymore. And she would be with me soon. He was right.

I should be silent. I should shush. I suddenly wanted to please him, to be the well-behaved girl I'd never, ever been. He wanted to bring me peace, and I would be a fool to interrupt his act of mercy.

It never occurred to me that the feelings weren't natural, but induced. Sure, I'd wished just about every day for the past three months for death to end my suffering and downward spiral, but I didn't want to be snuffed out by a red-eyed monster. I'd been considering something less dramatic, like a plummet from a bridge or a handful of pills. But comfort rolled from him like smoke, and I inhaled. And when something feels that wonderful—that pure—does it really matter if it's real or not?

"Shhh. You have my word, you will not suffer." His voice was deeply accented, purring, soothing. I sighed, letting my head loll to the side, a deep warmth suddenly sprouting in my belly and running through my limbs. I felt my half-numb lips twitching in the beginnings of a smile. His touch felt good, and though gravel was now pressing into my cheek, the pavement almost felt like a feather bed. My reaction seemed to please him, and his expression softened. He stroked my hair and cooed to me like I was a kitten that had done something adorable.

Then he was dragging me into the weeds just off the pavement by one arm as if I weighed nothing. Tall grass parted with a dry whisper, and I distantly watched some giant bug fly off into the night as we disturbed its resting spot. I was hauled into a sitting position, my head flopping like a doll's, then I felt his breath on my neck. I felt the tip of his tongue strike out, tapping along the delicate skin in a way that made me think of a nurse smacking her fingers against your arm as she searches for a vein to draw blood. Something stung there, two pinpricks of fire, and my arms twitched, but refused to rise and knock what felt like needles out of my skin. It was a combination I never wished to experience again, the sting of death and the warmth of pleasure. I wanted to kick, to scream, to run. The feeling

17

heightened to a sickening cramp and I wished I could ask him just to snap my neck and get it over with. But then it stopped, and suddenly I felt like someone had given me a morphine bath, the sting dying with the last of my willpower and fear. Pleasure flooded my frozen body, sucking and strumming every nerve and breathing molten ecstasy into every pore. If I could have snuggled into Red Eyes, I would have. I wanted to wrap my arms around him and pull him closer. I forgot about the argument with Aunt Mag and her wounded expression as I tore whatever shred of hope she hung onto into tiny, stringy pieces. I forgot about Steve, and the heat of his body and the raging hormones I'd played with for mean-girl kicks.

I forgot about Mom.

Life drained away and I welcomed it, my mouth filling with saliva as the craving for more became all I would ever be.

Then a lot of things happened at once. I heard a thump, and the sound of what could only be bones cracking. I fell weak and powerless to the ground, weeds suddenly obscuring my vision. I wanted to cry out, but not with fear. I was pissed and more hollow than I'd ever felt. It was like I'd caught a glimpse of heaven and the chariot leading me there had gotten a flat. The building desire was quickly dissipating and confusion took its place.

I heard a growl from my attacker and felt his cold presence spring away from my body. I tried to move, failed, and my sluggish brain felt like it was vibrating in my skull as it tried to make some sense of what was happening around me. I caught a glimpse of Red Eyes gliding through the air, and his fist popping out in a blur so fast I wasn't even sure I'd seen it at all. Another thump quickly followed, and I assumed he'd made contact with whatever he was rumbling with. I wondered if the newcomer was on my side, or if he was battling Red Eyes for first dibs of whatever he planned to take from me. I knew what everyone else would call Red Eyes if they were in my shoes. I'd watched dozens of horror movies starring his cousins, but I couldn't bring myself to accept the obvious.

I could hear the sounds of a struggle unfolding. Two people—or whatever the heck they were—grunted and breathed heavily. They were fighting to the death, if the hissing and the wet crackling of bone was any indication. The sound dug into my head and I wanted to cover my ears. I felt the terrible rolling that comes right before you realize you've drunk way too much, and tried to breathe in through my nose so I didn't hurl and draw any extra attention my way. Red Eyes danced into view, blond hair mussed and gleaming like spun gold in the moonlight, and the look on his face was that of total disbelief. He whispered in some guttural foreign language, his voice like ice and glass tinkling together. Somewhere a cricket chirped and something was crawling lazily beside my knee through the undergrowth I'd somehow become tangled in. Red Eyes' voice had sounded beautiful before, musical even, like waves crashing on a sunny, white-sanded beach. Now he sounded like a Russian serial killer. He was taking cautious, light steps backward, and was spinning to flee when something giant and the color of bleached bones flew through the air.

The giant snow-white wolf caught Red Eyes in the throat and they both went down in a tangle of white arms and fur. I heard a wet, meaty ripping sound and threw up in my mouth just a teensy bit when a cloud moved out of the way of the moonlight and illuminated the horrible scene unfolding before me.

Red Eyes didn't have a throat anymore, and liquid squirted in spurts from the wound. He gurgled, trying to lodge his long-nailed white fingers into the wolf's eyes, but the wolf shook his massive, furry head, snapping at Red Eyes' fingers. Red Eyes pulled back a squirting nub.

My tongue unfroze, and I sucked life-giving, fragrant air into my lungs. A few horrible seconds passed then the wolf was leaving Red Eyes and pouncing with purpose in my

19

direction. I suddenly wished that Red Eyes had finished the job. Being quietly preyed upon was one thing, but being ripped to pieces by the white beast was an entirely far more horrific way to go if the demonstration I'd just been given was any indication.

The beautiful, savage beast loomed above me and placed one massive paw almost gently on my belly as my body started to jerk and wake up. Something black and sulfuric smelling covered his maw, and I came dangerously close to peeing myself.

Then he was changing. Fur began to retract, the snout shortened then disappeared entirely. White furry ears shrank and became more human-like. It let out an almost human sigh, and I heard bones crackling and rearranging themselves as the massive white wolf became a boy who looked barely older than me.

And he was naked.

A now-human hand covered my mouth as I began to shriek hysterically. He shook his head and pushed the fingers from his other hand to his lips.

"Shut up. Now. Do you wanna be explaining to the cops why you're stoned and bleeding beside of the road? I'm here to help you, idiot!" he whispered angrily.

And the body, I thought, jerking my head in the direction of Red Eyes. Two seconds ago, a grotesque, lifeless monster had lain, there just feet away, but now the only thing I saw was something that sort of looked like baby powder puffing up on the breeze.

"He's gone! He's alive. Get off of me! He's going to kill me!" I shrieked.

He shook his head. "He was old and powerful, but there's nothing left. He's dead."

I pushed myself into a sitting position, and almost lay back down when a sharp pain shot through my neck. I lifted my trembling hand and placed my palm against the cool, uneven flesh. The skin stuck a little to my hand when I pulled it away and gaped at the wetness there. I looked down at my baby-blue tee, and my insides lurched in disapproval.

I don't think I'd ever seen so much blood on my person in my life, not even when I'd broken my nose in seventh grade during gym. The world blurred, and I trembled as I looked at the naked dude in front of me. Even unfocused, bleeding and dizzy, I resisted the urge to check him out below the waist as he crouched there like he'd never worn a stitch of clothing in his life with his elbows propped loosely on his knees. Soft waves of midnight-black hair curled along his brow. His strong nose was big without looking beakish, and his full, generous mouth was beginning to tighten in what looked like concern. He leaned in, actually sniffed me, and let out a string of curses that would have impressed me had I not been traumatized and possibly bleeding to death.

"Not good," he said with a voice both silky and husky at the same time. "You smell like sickness already." Little specks of light danced before my vision. His eyes kept me grounded for a few seconds longer—green with flecks of yellow around the pupil. They were bright, feverish, and flashed just for a second with something that wasn't even close to human.

"Home. Take me home. My house is that way." I tried to gesture behind me with a jerk of my head, but the action turned into a loll that sent me sinking back against the weedy earth.

Somewhere the cricket chirped again, not giving a fat damn about the scene unfolding before its beady, hard little eyes.

"You're coming with me," I heard him say before I drifted off on a black, blind storm cloud, with blazing-red eyes chasing me into what I figured was death.

Chapter Three

Misery

I was in hell and praying to God for forgiveness for my sins. Hot fire licked across every inch of my body, the burn eternal, relentless. I would have sold my soul for a drop of water. Once or twice, someone or something granted my request, but I choked on the life-giving fluid before it even had a chance to cool my melting, thick tongue. I visited memories I'd forgotten I had. Mom, driving me to school, yawning into her hand as she attempted to sing along with me as I belted *Mary Had A Little Lamb* from the backseat in a squeaky, high-pitched, trembling voice. I remembered Mom coming home after Grandma had died, staring at her hands in a daze as tears rolled off her cheeks. She regarded her palms as if she'd just used them to strangle a kitten, sobbing into the phone.

'I tried, Maggie. I didn't want to be the one to operate, but there was no one else. I was terrified I'd fail, and I did, Mag. She was too blocked, and she was more than halfway gone when they wheeled her in. What kind of doctor am I if I can't even save my own mommy?'

Five-year-old me had pressed my face into her hip, wiping at my eyes, not really understanding anything about what Mom was discussing with Aunt Mag, but knowing that Grandma had gone to heaven forever and ever and ever. I remembered staying up with Mom when I was twelve to watch *Child's Play,* and her laughter when we'd both jumped every time Chucky would pop his creepy little head out from a dark corner. I thought about Oz, my best friend since I'd been nine years old, and startled myself by wondering why I'd never kissed him.

Hell didn't only consist of fire and brimstone, but memories of people you'd never see again. The movie reel clicked on, showing scenes from my childhood, most of them wonderful. The more recent ones were horrible — Mom telling me she had cancer, Aunt Mag looking at me, desperate for comfort and a loved one to share her anguish with.

I started to moan, and soon it became a shriek. Someone kept grabbing my wrists with cool hands and I reached out, blind and shivering with raw, boiling pain, wanting more of their blessed chill. *Please,* I begged, *please hold me. Put out the fire. Please. Please. I'll be better if you'll just — Please, please.*

Two voices swam in and out of my head, one of them feminine and clipped. The voice belonged to the one in charge, sounding wise and ancient. The other voice was silky, masculine, and rose to frantic heights as it argued loudly with the other in words my overstimulated brain couldn't grasp. Then my eyes flew wide, clearing as they focused on the ceiling above me. It was rough looking, almost like plywood, and shadows danced from flames I could hear crackling somewhere nearby. As I lay there staring, my vision blurred in and out, then the ceiling opened. I stared wide-eyed and full of the childlike wonder only hard-core drugs can induce. I dragged in breaths of what felt like sand and tasted of blood as the gaping ceiling turned into a portal of color. From within the cotton-candy swirls of light, Red Eyes crept out. His head appeared first, fingers sticking to the ceiling as if the pads of them had little suction cups on the end. He hung upside down, legs bent, arching his head back. He grinned, blood that I instinctively knew as my own dripping from his mouth and onto my forehead. I shrieked.

My hands suddenly felt furry, my nails long and hooked. An electric tingle shot through me, strangely pleasant and contrasting with the agonizing kiss of flames on my skin. I

23

tried to scream as he dropped, but instead what came out was a chest-rumbling, savage roar. I felt a hand upon my chest, Red Eyes' long-nailed hand. The firelight danced in his eyes, reflecting my image—a reflection that wasn't human at all, but black and feline. I kicked, and my legs felt strangely arched. My mouth felt weird and wider, my teeth sharp and piercing my tongue. I lashed out at Red Eyes, but what went by my line of vision wasn't my hand, but a black paw. Red Eyes wavered like a mirage, then bent to my throat. The wound he'd given me throbbed and pulsated and I screamed again, but it wasn't a girl's scream. Hell, it wasn't even human. The sound that ripped from my burning throat was deep and guttural, feline and hair-raising. I roared at the dancing, spinning portal that Red Eyes would no doubt drag me into. He would drink and drink, until all that was left was the withered shell of a girl who hated herself more than any evil entity ever could. I laughed but made no sound. I laughed, but my lips never moved. The bubbling insanity never made it out, but Red Eyes could hear me. Yes, Red Eyes knew why I was laughing, because he threw back his beautiful head and laughed with me until my soul was floating like ash on the foul smelling waves of heat. My body still bucked and struggled in the tar coffin I'd believed to have been a bed moments before, and I shivered with the promise of the achingly close release that only he could grant me. I breathed brimstone and bits of crushed, ancient bone into my new lungs, and felt myself tumbling into the smoking inferno, a place where I belonged.

Soon, I gratefully descended into blackness again, thankful to be spared the second attack of Red Eyes, but not before a voice that tickled some distant memory sliced through.

"*Pearl! Pearl! Come quick!* She's shifting right here, *right now!* It's her true form...quick, before she shifts back!"

* * * *

24

I don't know how much time passed before I was back in what felt like a bed, but was cold like a river. The soft slab I writhed on was damp, and I convulsed and tore at the fabric beneath me. Hands once again pushed at my alien-feeling body, but I didn't feel the coolness. The blessed chill of hands never touched my bare skin, but the layer of something else above it. I heard ripping, felt my strange, furry fingers slice into the layers of my resting place.

Then I knew nothing.

* * * *

I woke to a cool glass being pushed to my lips, an ice cube bouncing against my teeth. "Drink," a female voice ordered, shaky, but with an unmistakable undercurrent of strength. It was the voice of a woman who was used to giving orders, and people following them without question.

"Umnaa?" I tried to ask where I was, but my head pounded something awful. Covers were tucked under my chin, and...wait...was I naked? I ran my hand down my bare side and discovered that—yes—I was as nude as the day I was born.

I opened my eyes, squinting at the sickeningly bright sunlight filtering cheerily through the window to my left. The woman before me studied me with watery, sky-blue eyes. One of her thin, gray brows arched. Silver curls sprang in every direction despite the tight bun atop her head. Blue-tinged lips were pressed in what looked like worry, but her thin, bird-like hand didn't tremble as it raised a cloth to my forehead, wiping on either side of my brow.

"Rough night, wuttin' it?" Her strong, slightly hoarse voice brought back fuzzy, violent memories that must have been dreams.

"How did I get here? What happened?" I asked, my own voice rough, my throat burning. I felt like I'd been chomping on razor blades all night. The old woman sighed. I pegged her for seventy if she were a day.

25

"I'm Pearl, if ya care to know." She lifted a brow and must have deemed my expression unsatisfying, because she huffed and looked as if she might spit in my direction. "Fine then, Jane Doe, I'll just call ya Unlucky then. Damn near got your fool self kilt! Might as well have been wearin' a flashin' sign around your neck that said 'Rape me and kill me, I'm stupid'!" She snarled, revealing small, surprisingly white teeth. She rolled her eyes heavenward. "Never would have seen me walking down no dark road by myself at your age. My daddy would have tanned my hide."

"My dad doesn't even know I exist, and my mother is dying. So if you're just gonna lecture me, please tell me where the hell I am so I can get my shit and leave." I looked away. I was going to kill Steve. He'd laced the weed with something a little too rich for my blood. I was pretty sure I'd been on my first-ever acid trip. I started to push myself up.

I was stunned into silence as a damp dishtowel flapped loudly against the side of my head. "Lay back down there. You ain't going nowhere until you answer some questions! I tend to ya all night while you're rantin' and ravin' and you wake up like you're too good for my hospitality? I saved your butt, youngin'. You'd be dead as a doornail without me and the least you can do is hold still for a bit." She was breathing heavily now, her many wrinkles deepening with outrage.

Okay. Freak. Weirdo. Whack job. Someone had gone rogue and the nursing home should be promptly notified of the crazy escapee wielding a dishtowel. I scooted as far as I could from her, thinking I'd really feel like shit if I had to sucker punch a senior citizen. But upon closer inspection, I had the suspicion that she wouldn't go down easily. Maybe it was the firm line of her thin lips, or the still-steady hand that held the dishtowel like a club, but mostly I think it was the way her eyes seemed to light up from within, a strange spark that faded so quickly I wasn't even sure I'd seen it at all.

26

I looked around the room. The walls were made of wide, unsanded logs, pieces of wood splintering in places. A fire blazed in a fireplace, bone-white stones making up the structure. The floors were, however, a beautiful gleaming cherry. A wicker rocking chair sat to one side of the bed and a dainty, marble nightstand on the other. A giant old dresser dominated the left side of the room, with dozens of whatnots and delicate little hand-painted lamps cluttering every bare surface below a huge oval mirror. Every picture on the walls were of flowers, pastel, and faded with age. I lay under a handmade quilt stitched with multicolored squares of different shades of blue. I sucked in a breath, pulled the covers to my exposed chest, and blurted the question that was probably the furthest from my mind.

"Where's my bra?"

The old woman tilted her head and gazed heavenward, mumbling something that sounded like a plea for the good Lord to kill her and put her out of her misery. Her shoulders slumped for just a second, then her back became straight once more. "You ripped clean out of it last night."

Wow, I thought, my cheeks flaming, *I ripped out of my bra in front of an old woman?* How does one even *do* that? Also, having no idea what transpired afterward was beyond horrifying. She must have seen my expression and she looked for a second like she would clarify but instead she visibly bit her tongue, evidently assuming that I deserved to wonder. Her watery blue eyes met mine steadily and she settled in, crossing her arms over her small bosom. I hadn't noticed it at first—her imposing personality must have thrown me off—but the woman was tiny, and I doubted she was ninety pounds soaking wet. You could tell her face had been pretty once upon a time, and still was underneath the disapproving frown that had been plastered to her face since the moment I'd seen her.

The fog was quickly dissipating. I was surprised by how fantastic I felt—physically stronger and healthier than I had been before my huge nightmare. And that was when it all hit

27

me—the details from the night before I'd been trying not to think about. Aunt Mag and her horrible news of my mother being a very short timer, my cruel reaction. Walking down the dark highway with soundless, inhumanly fast steps behind me. In my mind's eye, I felt the lure, the seduction of Red Eyes in all his terrible, moonlit glory. I remembered the white wolf with its muzzle dripping with the contents of Red Eyes' pale throat, and the strangely beautiful guy that it had shifted into. I also remembered all of the pain. So much pain.

My hand went to my throat, expecting to feel a bandage. I prodded the area where the nasty wound had been, and almost puked when I ran my fingertips across what felt like super smooth, barely puckered twin round scars.

"How long have I been here?" My voice sounded hollow, distant, on the verge of crumbling.

"Trace brought you here last night...you were pretty banged up. You're a very fortunate girl. Things could have been much worse. You need to count your lucky stars that you're gonna be livin' to witness another sunrise." She watched me carefully as I tried to make sense of everything. *Trace.* I repeated the name in my head, seeing if it rang some kind of bell.

"I...I must have had an accident. I remember being attacked by some guy, but it gets pretty blurry from there. I had a fight with my aunt...and I took a walk. Stupid, I know. Lesson learned." Aunt Mag would be frantic. The National Guard was probably swarming Perry—tiny as it was—and digging into every corner. I had no doubt my face was being printed on a milk carton somewhere. I looked around, spotted a small grandfather clock on the dresser. Six a.m. If I left right then, I'd have just enough time to beg a ride home from some passing motorist and devise some half-believable story to explain my all-nighter to Aunt Mag. Of course, she'd assume I was at some sex party and participating in some marathon orgy with male strippers, but I might survive.

I thought of Mom and my stomach lurched. What if she wasn't there when I got home? *Don't think about it, Wren,* the voice inside self-soothed. *She's gone anyway. Your mother isn't there anymore. She's just a shell. You've already grieved her death. You've gotten that out of the way. No matter that she's still breathing – she died weeks ago.*

Tears burned in my eyes and I swung my bare legs from the bed. "I've got to go!" I snapped a little frantically, grabbing a folded, white, too-large tee and baggy gray sweatpants from the nightstand that I assumed were meant for me. "My mom...she's really sick, and I need to leave now. Can someone...drive me home?"

Her eyes narrowed and she stood along with me as I clutched the quilt to my chest. "Can't drive. Never did. You'll have to get Trace to give you a lift."

I turned on my heel, yanking the tee over my head and shimmying into the sweats. Thankfully my shoes had survived the night and I bent to grab them from the floor that was clean enough to eat off. The boy she was referring to had to be the one who I'd imagined was a white wolf the night before.

"Trace?" I played dumb.

"Yes. Trace is my godson. He's the one who found you last night. He's in the kitchen, and if you'll wait a minute I'll fetch him."

I nodded and watched her leave with her steady, seemingly pain-free gait.

As soon as the thick oak door clicked softly behind her, I was running for the window. I'd forgotten to ask exactly where I was. I didn't even know if I was still in Perry County, but I wasn't risking another meeting with the dude who had brought me here. I knew that I couldn't have seen what I thought I had last night. Obviously a great percentage of it was some super-detailed hallucination, but imagining of seeing him again made me extremely uneasy.

I ran to the window, unlocked it with a click, and peered out. Good – looked like there was only one level and no

29

high drop involved. I swung one leg out then the other, getting a small splinter in my thigh in the process. I landed in a rosebush, some of its delicate petals puffing out into the morning breeze as my feet hit the muddy earth. A battered blue Chevy pickup sat maybe ten feet away on a white gravel driveway. I was wondering if the keys were inside, and thinking of the possibilities when I heard the door swing open to the room I'd just escaped. I took off at a dead run, and almost cried out with disappointment when I realized how far back in the sticks I was. The road turned from gravel into a deeply rutted, rocky trail barely wide enough for a truck. It didn't seem possible that the road saw daily traffic. Gravel bounced down the steep incline as I slid to a stop and I prayed my ankles would hold for the treacherous run.

There was no way in hell I was going back. I was sure Granny Applesmith was preparing her oven and sharpening her knives as her godson revved up his chainsaw, and I wasn't about to stick around for dinner. I had to get home. I had to see my mother. What if I was too late?

"Damn it," I panted, hopping from rock to rock on my way down and busting my butt on a slick one. I stopped, my backside throbbing, listening for the sound of traffic ahead. One look, and I'd know my location. I knew the road's curves better than the curves of my body. Insects sang and squirrels squawked their displeasure as I loudly picked my way as fast as I could off the mountain. Five minutes and one scraped knee later I was greeted by the sweet noise of a car that needed a muffler. I'd made it.

I was straining my neck and trying to get a visual when I heard a loud growl. At first I thought it was my stomach protesting its lack of breakfast, but the sound just got louder. Freezing, I turned slowly, feeling a powerful presence almost physically stir the air around me. But I saw nothing.

I was turning back, planning on running the rest of the way to the main road, when warm air *whooshed* around me. Eyes that I'd seen both in the head of an animal and the face of a beautiful boy met mine, glinting with obvious displeasure. It was the white wolf, and no doubt he'd be chomping at my neck like he had Red Eyes' in my nightmare the night before.

Daylight did the animal no favors, and the almost blinding white of his fur bristled underneath my gaze. Paws as big as Frisbees sank into the muddy earth of the trail, and ears with tufts of white fur at the tips twitched as if my slamming heart was audible and too loud for his tastes. His heavily furred, thick tail swished low to the ground and he flashed a muzzle full of razor-sharp fangs at me soundlessly. It was almost a dang grin.

I gave the squirrels something to squawk about all day as I screeched and bolted toward the road. Nothing pursued, and I sobbed with relief when I reached pavement, bending double and bracing my hands on my knees as I gasped for air and tried to calm myself before I hyperventilated. It didn't take me long to score a ride, and the old man with no teeth and a red trucker's hat didn't give my trembling hands a second glance as I gripped the dashboard all the way home. I hopped out with a muttered thanks, took the porch steps by twos, and before my hand could touch the knob, Aunt Mag was flinging it open. She looked me over roughly, breathed deeply through her nose, and sagged against the doorframe.

"She's still alive, on the off chance that you're interested. The hospice folks are with her now." She was trying her best to come off as scornful, but only managed to sound as sad and tired as she looked. I gulped, dropping my head and almost falling on my face as I reached to tug off my mud-caked shoes on the inside mat.

"I'm sorry, Mag, I-I got into a bit of a mess, but it's all better now. I didn't mean to be a — "

"Hateful, selfish brat?" she finished for me.

I pursed my lips and nodded, swiping at my eyes before any tears leaked out. I'd give her that one, I deserved it, but I wished like hell she hadn't verbalized how awful I'd been for the last few weeks. I didn't look up, and was ready to creep away when she grabbed me.

But this time it wasn't out of anger, it was out of understanding—something I didn't deserve. She pulled me to her chest, the Santa Claus on her red tee way out of season, and propped her chin on my head. Aunt Mag was tall, whopping six-foot even, and she towered over my five-foot-four frame. The dam broke and I cried into her shoulder, taking in great big gulps of her comforting scent: fabric softener and jasmine perfume.

"It's gonna be all right. It can't be this bad forever," she told me, the words comforting, but she sounded as if she really didn't even believe it herself.

I managed a muffled whisper into her shoulder. "No, it's not."

Aunt Mag gently took my shoulder, stepping back until she could meet my eyes. "I know it feels that way at the moment, and it may for a long time, but we've gotta be strong now, Wren. She'd kick our butts if she saw us moping like this."

I sighed, hearing the soft, gossipy chatter of the two nurses who had been making daily visits with my mother so they could assist her in her inevitable passing. I could have said a million negative things in response to that comment, and part of me wanted to, but I didn't.

Later, when the nurses had cleared, I sat by my mom's bedside watching her chest rise and fall. I brushed her pale-blonde hair, rubbed lotion on the dry, cracking hands that had helped so many live better lives, and felt incredibly sorry for myself. I tried not to look at the catheter bag. I tried not to notice the smell that all sick rooms seem to possess no matter the disinfectant, and in a low whisper recounted my night. I knew she couldn't hear me, but I figured that if I described the events out loud, they'd make a little more sense. Of course, they didn't.

I couldn't seem to shake the shivering chill that had seeped into my bones since my encounter with the red-eyed nightmare. My mom was dying, that would be enough stress to induce horrible hallucinations, but the thought didn't comfort me. By the time I'd kissed her cheek and fluffed her pillows, I was pretty certain I'd gone off the deep end.

I climbed the creaking stairs, pulling at the rails as my body began to give in to exhaustion. I stumbled into my room, blowing a half-hearted kiss at my Thirty Seconds to Mars poster, and collapsed onto my twin mattress. I tossed the decorative, annoying pillows into the corner and curled under the dark-brown comforter, rolling onto my side to stare at the picture on the white nightstand. Mom's beautiful, happy face grinned from a five-by-seven picture we'd taken together last year. Her soft, storm-gray eyes sparkled with an inner light she carried everywhere she went. Mom's best friend runs a photography business, so Mom usually dragged me with her a few times a year to immortalize ourselves and give her girlfriend a chance to try new photography techniques risk-free. In the picture, I looked pretty happy too. My hair was just a bit too frizzy, my dimples just a little too pronounced to be considered womanly, but my face had an expression that said safe, secure.

The cordless trilled loudly, causing me to jump. I pushed Talk and was greeted with a sigh I recognized immediately.

"Your aunt was freaking out. Where the hell were you? I drove all over town looking for you. I even checked the gutter, which is exactly where you seem to stay lately. What the frig, Wren? I can never reach you anymore. I thought we were besties?" Oswald Jacobs — Oz for short, if you wanted to live — grumbled. I could see him pacing and throwing darts at the board on the wall above his bed. More often than not he forgot to remove the darts, and slept under them. I kept waiting for him to have to have one surgically removed from his eye.

With his shaggy blond hair that always stayed over his big brown eyes, his wide, full mouth and his tiny, pert nose, he was adorable. Adorable in that I-just-want-to-pinch-his-cheeks kind of way. He'd sprouted up a couple of years ago, but had only succeeded in looking thinner and growing barely a shadow of a beard. I envied his creamy skin, but he seemed intent on puncturing as many holes in it as he could. Within the last six months he'd pierced his lip, his eyebrow and his tongue. He said the ladies liked it, but I figured it was his way of proving that he wasn't entirely a pansy.

I groaned, rolling over and pulling a pillow over my face as I cradled the phone against my ear with my shoulder. "For the love of God, do not pull this auntie crap on me right now. I'm not even gonna go into it, so don't ask. And the door swings both ways, Oz. You haven't stopped by in at least a week. You know things are crazy around here right now."

And that was all it took. He never stayed mad at me for more than an hour. A long-winded, dramatic sigh, and I heard his bed creak through the receiver as he plopped down. He was probably running his hand through his bangs. God, I missed him.

"Sorry, Wren. I know you've got a lot going on, it's just… I know were out with him, and we both know what a jerk he can be." Something changed in his voice on the last few words, making them sound more bitter than he normally did. Oz hated Steve. Amazingly, aside from a few snide remarks exchanged in passing in the hallways at school aimed toward Oz, and one locker incident, the two didn't have much beef with each other. Sure, Steve was an ass, but Oz had never really given him more than a shrug until now.

"He's not like that. He's a pussycat. Should have seen him last night… I practically preformed a castration on my lawn." I forced a giggle. I waited for Oz to laugh with me, but was greeted with silence. We never had awkward moments, but I was thinking I was experiencing one of our first.

34

Then he spoke. "It's not really Josh I'm worried about, Wren, it's you. You know what I'm talking about. I'm here. You know that, right? If you need anything, anytime, I'm here. Can I come over tonight? I'll bring my console and we can play Call of Duty."

I didn't want to see anyone. I wanted to stay in bed until I heard the cries of Aunt Mag that would signify my mom's passing and wail with her until my throat bled. I wanted to curl into a ball and smoke so much weed I'd never be straight again. I was mad at God, confused by my hallucinations, and way worried about whatever had happened to me last night. I couldn't make sense of anything, and I wondered what I'd really been doing if Red Eyes hadn't been biting me in the field. Wandering around with the mosquitoes in the middle of the woods? Interacting with road signs? What?

I opened my mouth to tell him no, that it wasn't a good idea, that I was tired and not feeling well, but then I reached up to cup my neck. If someone had poured ice water on me the effect wouldn't have been as jolting. Two smooth, slightly puckered circles were hot under my hand, and as I pressed, they ached and the muscle below spasmed. The vein just under the skin throbbed painfully as my blood roared through my head. I almost screamed, a stone forming in my belly as my teeth began to chatter softly.

Then I knew. I couldn't do this alone. Not anymore.

"Yeah," I told Oz, my voice barely a whisper. "Tonight will be great."

* * * *

The boy sat in front of the fireplace listening to the old woman chant as she sliced her palm with a large, leather-hilted dagger. She tossed the blood into the fire, her eyes rolling back into her skull until all that was visible were the whites, now slightly yellow with age. Her body shuddered once, twice, then went still. Her thin, slight form slumped

35

back against the wooden rocking chair, her arm flopping to the side. While the blood had flowed freely from the self-inflicted wound mere seconds before, now it was just a steady drip. Trace wanted to ask her about the girl he'd been watching again. Pearl had told him all she knew, of course, but talking about the chestnut-haired beauty with the stunning aqua eyes soothed him in a way he couldn't explain.

Pearl had taken him under her wing nearly fifty years prior, announcing that she was adopting him lest he become a savage.

"A man needs a woman around, someone to mother him. Don't matter how old he is, a man just can't take care of himself for long periods alone. Ain't no use in you runnin' back and forth every day for information or help when you can just stay here and keep an old woman company."

Trace still didn't know Pearl's true age, and he had the feeling he never would. She'd looked the same for as long as he could remember, her skin neither sagging more visibly nor tightening into a more youthful texture. Pearl just *was*, and no one questioned her abilities. Most of the otherworlders regarded her with the same reverence and awe they would reserve for the president. She was wise and gentle, her sweet, grandmotherly appearance misleading. Trace knew that Pearl could make herself look less fragile if she chose, for it was rumored — and he believed it — that she was one of the oldest witches in the country. Pearl could have made everyone see whatever he or she wanted when they looked at her, but she preferred the old, wrinkled body she seemed to have grown quite attached to, even hobbling with her hand on the small of her back as if it ached around humans who would expect such from a feeble old lady. She could heal with a touch, and in the same breath, kill without mercy. He'd seen magic dancing in her hands, creating miracles and curing everything from cancer to demonic possession in those she chose to bless, and he'd witnessed those very hands curl into sharp-nailed claws, pointing with a hex and a mumbled word, causing men to bleed from their eyes and beg at her feet for the mercy of death. He was eternally grateful that he was on her nice list.

He also wasn't sure when he'd began to think of her as his mother, but as he stared at her deceptively fragile-looking form lying limp in the dancing shadows by the firelight, he felt his heart tug.

He figured Pearl probably knew the small secret he'd been keeping, she always did, but she hadn't let on.

He had somehow become emotionally confused by the girl he'd been ordered to only study and, if necessary, protect.

He'd watched the girl the night before, resisting the urge to burst the glass on that ridiculous vehicle the tall, mannerless boy had planned to bed her in. After Trace watched her tease the idiot man-child with kisses until he'd been pleading for release, Trace had found himself worked into a fury he didn't really understand. Trace had easily heard every foolish word they'd uttered from his hiding spot even though the doors and windows were shut tight and the Jeep's engine had been idling. What was wrong with him? Why did he feel such an intense desire to hurt the boy for touching the foolish girl? He'd heard their breathing become heavier, then the telltale fumbling and whisper of fabric rustling. He'd stood up then, moving slowly toward the Jeep in a crouch, silent and confident that the cloaking spell Pearl had cast for him had been doing its job. It had been just as he'd thought, Wren had been removing her shirt. The boy had trailed a line of sloppy kisses down her slim white throat. Her long black lashes had swept her cheeks as she closed her eyes, her full lips pouty and slightly parted. Her oval, alabaster face had been tilted up, her long chestnut hair spilling in glossy waves down her back that managed to shine even with the artificial lighting in the Jeep's interior. He'd been ready to stop her then for reasons he couldn't quite explain, to drag her out, demand that she clothe herself, and punch the boy she toyed with

37

until he bled from his ears, but he'd held back. The girl didn't know what she was. The girl wasn't his to control. Who was he to interfere?

He'd known that he had gone far beyond investigating. He'd known that he was invading the girl's privacy, yet he hadn't been able to walk away. The pain she carried like a stone was plainly visible, even when she smiled and laughed and drank and smoked herself into numb cheerfulness. For weeks now he'd watched, and he knew all too well what was happening. He wanted to help, to soothe, to shake her until her teeth rattled and make her see what she was capable of, but instead he'd kept his distance, minding Pearl's warnings not to let himself be seen.

His fists had tightened, and he'd considered punching through the glass, yanking the boy out of the vehicle by his ears and throwing the girl over his shoulder and escorting her back to her frantic, depressed aunt. And even though it didn't make sense, all Trace had been able to think of when he'd looked at the girl who was slowly becoming something she had no idea even existed was...

Mine.

The tall, fair-haired boy with an artificial tan had gripped the girl's back hungrily, his fingers sliding over the smooth, unmarked skin. He'd fumbled with the clasp of her black, lacy bra.

Trace had seen red, and concluded that whatever Pearl had ordered no longer mattered. He'd tried to place the disturbing sensation digging into his gut, and it had taken him a bit of searching to find the right word to explain his emotions. Finally it had hit him, a name for that alien emotion he hadn't experienced since his youth, and even then, very briefly.

Jealousy.

He was horrified and disgusted, but it still didn't quell the rage.

Then something glorious had happened, and Trace had felt a relief so profound that he'd almost allowed himself to

38

lean against the passenger side door. The girl had laughed, and the sound had held no joy. Instead…

"Oh, please. You aren't getting into my pants here. What the hell is that playing, anyway? Please, for the love of God, tell me that isn't Alan friggin Jackson."

The idiot boy had looked like a puppy that had been whacked with a newspaper. He'd picked up the fat joint that had still been smoldering in the ashtray, and had almost missed his lips as he lifted it to his mouth, eyes wide in disbelief, but trying desperately hard to pretend he was unfazed by her rejection as she'd coldly slipped her blue T-shirt back over her head.

"I've told you," she'd said a little breathlessly. "I don't do cars, or trucks, or rigs, or anything else that has an engine. I need a bed, and not the one at your mama's house. I need a hotel room—no, a suite, with a mini fridge full of booze and a Jacuzzi."

She'd rambled on, adding more ridiculous requirements and slipping the joint from the hand of the boy whose face was transforming quickly from disbelief to annoyance. His handsome, soft features had shifted into something ugly, as if he could have happily tossed her from the top of the mountain where they'd been parked. With a tensed jaw, he'd yanked the gearshift into Drive and spun his tires as he'd whipped the Jeep around, barely missing Trace's left side with the bumper. Trace had easily danced away, graceful and lithe, blending once again into the shadows. Soon he'd been high above the Jeep, gliding and enjoying the way the wind slipped like warm silk over the graceful lines of his wings. Wren had been going home. She'd had her fun, she'd gotten stoned as usual, and had kissed and wounded her second boy that week. He'd see that she made it safely indoors, and would leave her to her sadness, but even as he'd told himself this, he'd known he'd linger just outside her home, listening to the floors creak as she paced them, or to her crying when she'd managed to evade her aunt long enough to lock herself in her room. She'd wake, of course, to slip downstairs several times during the night to check on her mother. Trace would watch her sleep, always fitfully, and would wish that he could smooth her hair from her damp brow as she mumbled and thrashed. He noticed she had more nightmares if she went to sleep high. But that night had been different. Instead of hiding in her room, a fight with her aunt had prompted Wren to take a late-night stroll. When the vampire had attacked her, Trace had held back, circling overhead, wondering if her terror would cause her to shift for the first time. It *hadn't,* and she'd been bitten, something he felt guilty over, but he knew she'd never been close to death. Enduring a bite was painful, excruciatingly so, but she'd healed quickly, as he'd known she would.

* * * *

He was drawn like a moth to a flame, so much so that he could never tell Pearl, lest she think him incompetent and smitten. He was smitten, yes, but it was much more than that.

He knew that even though they had never spoken to one another, he would die for the girl if necessary.

Pearl moaned from her place in front of the fire, and purple sparks crackled at her worn fingertips. She appeared to be dreaming, but he knew that she was communicating with someone, or something. He shivered as he recalled the troll she'd been having tea with earlier. He had intended to discuss the girl's future with Pearl, but she'd been too focused on preparations for her trance.

"Later," she told him, a strange catch in her voice. "Bad things are afoot, son, and I have to get all o' my ducks in a row. You'd best be gettin' back to the girl before long. She'll be like a beacon now that she's bloomin', and it's untellin' what might decide to pay her a visit. The good Lord will keep her safe, though, ain't got a doubt in my mind."

That was another thing that he found peculiar about Pearl

but never questioned—her faith.

She went to church on Sundays, he'd even gone along once, but she'd remained silent throughout the sermon, only nodding occasionally. Trace knew that if the small Baptist church knew just what she was, she would no longer be welcome, but no one asked, and Pearl didn't tell. She had a Bible on her nightstand and so did Trace, although his was smaller and not nearly as worn as Pearl's.

A Jehovah's Witness had made it up to the cabin once and Pearl had, surprisingly, invited him in for tea.

"What do you believe, ma'am?" the old black man had asked, and even Trace had been able to sense the goodness and something that felt strangely holy almost shimmering about him.

"I believe the good Lord died for our sins. I got a lot of sins. You don't get this old without sinnin' just about any way there is to do it. But I also believe that he's not the uptight dictator we paint him as. He gave us rules, yes, but he also gave us amazing gifts—gifts a lot of folk say are sinful. I use what he gave me. I do what I feel is right. I talked to a goddess the other day in my hallway, and I trapped a demon in a teapot and boiled it into a harmless vapor. What do you say to that, sir?"

The man had left in a hurry, flabbergasted. Trace thought that the man had genuinely believed Pearl had been being cruel and mocking him, but Pearl had even seemed a bit disappointed.

"Was just trying to strike up some conversation then he ran like the devil was at his heels. Handsome gent, he is. Nice voice, too. Ain't seen an aura that pretty on a man since I was a girl. Oh my word...*that voice*... I'd listen to him recite the dictionary with a voice like that."

But Trace was thinking of another voice as he stared into the uncomfortably hot fire blazing in the fireplace.

He shot to his feet, almost pressed a kiss to Pearl's forehead, then caught himself. He'd disturbed her in a trance only once, and he'd never again make the same foolish error.

41

Having his clothing burst into flame right on his ass was not something he wanted to experience more than once.

The girl wasn't in immediate danger, he knew, because he would have sensed it, but he didn't want to take a chance. He reached into the pocket of his sandblasted jeans and felt for the lock of hair. It made him feel a little bit like a creep, and to anyone else he would have possibly been labeled a pervert, but he dug it out and lifted it to his nose nonetheless.

It smelled of lavender and mountain air, with the faint coppery smell of her blood. The chestnut color caught the light from the fireplace, and shone with almost crimson highlights.

Pearl had snipped it off and given it to him when the girl had been fighting for her life, caught in between Blooming and human and still experiencing the effects of a vampire bite as most humans would.

But the beast had pulled through.

He snapped on the thick-chained locket Pearl had given him that she claimed was good luck, and nestled the lock of hair inside. He bent and let it fall cool and loose around his neck. Then he was out the front cabin door and shifting into his wolf, feeling her presence grow stronger with every step.

* * * *

I'd wanted to nap. I felt weird and achy all over. I kept catching whiffs of scents I couldn't identify and my body thrummed with a jittery restless energy that made me feel like running, and running and running. I got up to jog downstairs and check on Mom once, not seeing any change, and shared a Coke with Aunt Mag while she watched some eighties movie I couldn't place. I knew I should have felt awful. I should have been exhausted, but the longer I stayed awake, the more restless I felt. I thought of the old strange woman who had taken me into her home sometime

42

during my wild psychedelic night, and the godson whom I'd imagined had been a large white wolf. I wondered what she thought of me, or if she had had called the police after I'd left to report a missing, emotionally troubled teen.

Around four p.m. I was succeeding in winding down, even though my bones felt electrified and my head was swimmy. I pulsed in and out of wakefulness, mostly staying in that in-between place that is neither awake nor asleep, and rolled until my sheets were a tangled mess at my feet.

I'm not sure when my body finally gave up the good fight, but I must have dozed pretty hard because when I woke, it was to a room of inky blackness. The mouse on my desktop computer glowed faintly green from its small LED light. The room was otherwise dark and cool, and I usually liked it that way, but tonight it just gave me the creeps.

Then I heard it—

Tap tap...tap.

I managed to not bolt upright and shriek. I was afraid it would wake Mom from her sometimes-coma and scare her into an even earlier death, not to mention Aunt Mag would run to my room with a lamp or an umbrella, ready to clobber a vandal. Her weepy, soft grief was very misleading—the woman had a tough streak a mile long.

My legs and feet—of all things—began to tremble, and I scrunched both sets of toes together to still them. My fingers were ice against my belly, and I slowly turned my head in the direction of my window, the soft glow of the street lamp casting buttery light over the carpet underneath it.

Nothing.

I let out the breath I'd been holding and my stomach sank like a popped balloon, my chest burning with fear. I hadn't been fully awake, had I? And the farmhouse was old. Just like an elderly person with joints that begin to creak louder over time, the house was announcing its age as it settled, maybe even sighing for the stressed, sad beings it sheltered.

I was just begging to relax a bit when I heard it again, slightly louder this time.

Tap tap...tap...tap.

I couldn't help it, I rose into a sitting position like a spring was attached to my back. I heaved the covers away from my body, throwing my legs off the side of the bed opposite of the window, and prepared to bolt for the door. To hell with cowering and waiting for some weirdo to shatter my window with his fist. My first instinct was to scream for Mom, and I actually took the breath before I remembered. In spite of the fear, a dull pang poked at my heart. Aunt Mag was at the end of the hall, and I was pretty sure I'd get there before whoever it was made their way in. I looked behind me as I rose to my feet. That was a mistake.

The thing tapping at my window didn't have eyes, or even a nose. I could only see its head, a head that reminded me of the top of a whole pickle. Thick, sausage-like lips were pulled back in an impossibly wide grin, revealing pointed layers of toothpick-sized teeth. It was breathing heavily, and each time it exhaled from its hideous maw, its breath fogged the glass. Shadowed, vaguely human fingers with little suction cups on the ends tapped more persistently and the thing wiggled with what looked like almost canine excitement. The world tipped weirdly, a scream rising to get stuck in my throat.

As I watched, the abomination's grin tipped up a little more at its corners and the places where its eyes should have been began to leak with some dark-colored fluid that dripped onto its fingers. A faint keening noise rose, then something that sounded like the chirp of a dying bird whistled into the night. A fat, leathery tongue slipped out from between its horrible teeth and made circular movements on the glass. I turned to run, but never made the step forward. The last thing I recall was my eggshell carpet getting closer to my face.

Chapter Four

Awakening

Someone shook me roughly and my eyes flew open. My hand shot out, clasped something soft and warm, and squeezed. A noise like distant thunder was vibrating in my chest and made its way out from between my clenched teeth.

Oz stared back, big blue eyes wide, clawing at my hand as it constricted his windpipe. Bright-red splotches of color stood out on his creamy skin and the glow of the street lamp outside my window reflected off the ring at the corner of his lower lip.

I let go, confused and horrified, and Oz took a deep, starving lungful of breath. He was struggling to breathe normally as I sputtered apologies, running my hands over his shoulders and assuring myself that he was fine. How could I have done such a thing? How had I managed to choke a tall, wiry boy twice my size with one hand?

Oz shook his head, and when he spoke his voice was hoarse and maybe just a little afraid, "What...in the hell... was that?"

"I don't know!" I shouted, covering my lower face with my hands. He seemed to recover, shushed me, then pushed my hair out of my eyes.

"Don't yell! Your aunt will think I'm up here ravishing you or something." He wasn't treating me like I'd just choked him until his cheeks were mottled red. Oz stood, offering his hand. After he'd assisted my shaking body over to sit at the edge of the bed, he flicked on my bedside lamp. The shadows slid quickly into the farthest corners of the room and I turned my head to stare at the window, which reflected the lamplight back along with the outline of a bustling Oz. He grabbed my robe, handed it to me wordlessly, and plopped down beside of me while I slipped into the cool fabric.

I didn't expect the question, "Are you doing drugs, Wren?"

Amazingly, I laughed. I laughed so hard I snorted, pressing my face into his shoulder. He went totally still, letting me get the mirth out of my system, then craned his neck.

"Talk to me, Wren."

I stared at him, reached out to push the too-long bangs out of his eyes, and pressed my lips together until they went numb. After a few more uncomfortable seconds had passed I answered, "No, Oz. It's ridiculous that you'd even entertain that thought."

I tried to give him my best chilly glare, but his expressive, concerned face didn't change.

"Want to tell me what you were doing unconscious out on the floor then?" he asked.

I dropped my head, knowing that I could trust him with anything, anything at all, but this stuff wasn't your normal run-of-the-mill teen drama. I wasn't upset because a boy had dumped me. I didn't have an eating disorder. My mother was dying, and demonic-looking things were licking my bedroom window at night.

I fell into the words like stepping from a ledge. If I'd thought harder about how they would sound, I would have chickened out. "Something weird is happening to me. I-I'm seeing things that aren't there. Things are trying to hurt me."

I could almost see his heart in his throat, and felt like blubbering like an idiot as he pulled me close, stroking my hair. I remembered believing that Red Eyes would kill me, and how I'd wondered why I'd never kissed Oz. I had no idea how I was supposed to feel about that weird, fleeting thought. I was melting against him, ready to spill the whole thing, when he said the dreaded words no psycho wants to hear.

"We'll get you some help, Wren. I'm here for you, just like I said on the phone earlier. Someone to talk to… Things will get better."

I would rather have had him set fire to my robe and put out the flame with his urine. But could I even blame him? He thought I was crazy. Okay. Yeah. That was pretty much understandable, but for some reason it still stuck sideways in my craw.

I pushed away and leveled him with my trademark glare, crossing my legs and letting my hands fist in my lap. I knew I looked like a pouting thirteen year old who'd been told she couldn't go to a party with boys, but I didn't care. "Right, Oz, I'm stressed and it just makes sense that I'm seeing shit, right? I mean, I never knew my dad, and my mom is dying a horrible death, and I don't really have any friends anymore, so it all kinda fits together like a big, tear-soaked puzzle." I took a deep breath, jerking my head toward the door. "Aunt Mag didn't escort you up? What if I had been naked? You think it's okay to walk in without knocking?"

Immediately I just felt like I'd dropped a bag of newborn kittens into a raging river. He winced, ran his hand through his lovely locks and sheepishly ducked his head to play with his lip ring. "Your aunt let me in and, I don't know, she looked upset, like she'd been crying. She just kinda shooed me up. I knocked, and I thought you might be asleep but, I don't know. Something just felt…wrong, so came in and found you on the floor."

I laughed. "Felt *wrong*? I guess you're psychic now, huh? Right. And I'm the crazy one." I walked over to my window, staring out at the black, looming Appalachians. Moths flitted outside the pane smacking the glass like fat, fuzzy bullets while they tried desperately to reach the light inside.

I looked down and noticed that the local stray was trying to make its way into the garbage bin outside. I left kibble for him every night, but he still insisted on raiding our trash. He was terrified of humans, and before Mom had gotten bedridden she'd made it her mission to pet him at least once. She'd done better than that, she'd made him fall in love with her, and some nights she had sat out on the front porch and petted him and petted him, as she stared out into the darkness. He wouldn't come near me. I'd even witnessed Frogger chasing him away once, butting him with his sturdy horns right in the rump.

Tonight, the dog growled. I couldn't hear it, but I could see his teeth pulled back from his long, flea-bitten brown snout. Just a mutt of a dog, a scrap of a thing. Part poodle and part something even uglier. Tonight he lay at a sort of crouch in front of our house, growling and twitching his head. To a passerby he might even appear rabid, that was if they couldn't see what we both obviously could.

The monster was back, and standing just below the streetlight. I could see that it was wearing clothes, and though torn and tattered, they covered it totally. Its collared, dingy white shirt was tucked into black trousers. Big, mud-caked brown boots covered feet, small in comparison to the rest of its wide frame. It was tall, and I guessed blankly that it would tower above me at a near eight feet in height. It might have passed for human from the neck down if not for its long, dark-green suction cup fingers. The bumpy, green head, missing eyes and ears, and a nose tipped backward and turned in the direction of my window. Its razor teeth became more visible as the skin pulled back in what I guess was supposed to be a grin. It lifted its hand, fingers moving one by one in a slow, wiggling wave.

It had come back for me.

I clutched at my robe, telling myself I would not back away. Something low rumbled in my chest and suddenly I could hear Oz rambling on, and he sounded so, so loud.

48

I could smell the apple-scented air freshener plugged in across, and the fragrance was so overwhelming that I gagged. My back felt like it was rippling, and not just with fear. No, the fear was there, but something else was quickly overriding it. Rage. Rage, disgust and something that felt vicious and animalistic. I gritted my teeth. I wanted to run downstairs, throw open the door, and tear into the ugly, monstrous hallucination with my claws. I wanted to jump on its back and shove my fingernails into the places where its awful eyes should have been and send it back to whatever nightmare hell it had come from.

"Oz, come here."

Whatever he was saying, which I was guessing was more psychobabble about my wounded little heart and how he would be my best friend forever and ever to cry on if I needed it, stopped.

"O-kay. What is it? Is it that poor dog again?" I heard the bed creak as he lifted himself from the mattress. And suddenly his scent hit me, a mixture of cheap body spray that promised to make the chicks go wild in a fit of a lust, and the metallic tang of sweat that for some reason made me believe he was nervous. I had no idea how I could smell him so strongly, but I did. Some other scent wafted to my nose and I nearly gagged on the aroma of sickly sweet decay. I also detected a sharp note of anger in the scent that made my nostrils flare in agitation. I didn't think it was coming from Oz, but I had no time to wonder about that bit of weirdness. I kept my eyes on the green thing in the human clothes below. The stray was still growling, bouncing forward a bit and snapping only to retreat closer to the house. It was almost as if he was defending his turf, and maybe, just maybe, the human who had petted him when no one else would. I wondered if he had a name. If Mom had given him one, I'd never paid enough attention to her chatter to notice, and somehow that struck me as more frightening than the thing smiling up at me from my front yard.

I felt Oz beside me and his scent got stronger. Under normal circumstances I would have told him to go take a shower and asked if he'd jogged over rather than driven, but instead I reached out and took his warm hand in mine.

"Look." I pointed to the creeper below the streetlight. The thing's attention hadn't wavered, and as I pointed he did a quick, sure little spin on the ball of one foot. He began to tilt his head from side to side and gestured to the place on its fleshy, sagging wrist where a watch would be if he'd had one.

Tick…tock…tick…tock.

The message was clear. I was running out of time, and it wouldn't be long before he crawled through my window and gnawed me into the afterlife.

I repressed a shiver, holding on to the rage making my forehead bead with cold sweat. I could see Oz staring at me from the corner of my vision. He didn't release my hand, but he bounced awkwardly from foot to foot. He was uncomfortable, but wasn't screaming, so it was safe to say he wasn't seeing what I was seeing.

"Wonder what he's growling at? I don't see anything… probably a fox or something," he said, his voice weirdly low, some emotion I couldn't place echoing on the notes. My heart sank, but I didn't tell him what I'd been pointing at. Even if I was crazy, I wasn't going to confirm it.

"Yeah, probably."

Suddenly the razor-toothed thing backed up, and from the quick, little hitches of its chest and the twitching of its thick, rubbery lips, I guessed it was laughing. Then it was gone. One moment it was slowly backing away from the light and the next it was just…gone. As I turned from the window and dropped Oz's hand, I heard the stray howl. My heart squeezed and I trembled. The sound pretty much summed up everything I was feeling—it was full of fear, grief and rage.

* * * *

I spent the next couple of hours watching some godawful romantic comedy with Oz, which had somehow become tense and weirdly embarrassing over the course of the evening. Things had never been awkward between us, so I wondered what had changed. Oz actually reddened during the kissy-face scenes and scooted closer to me once or twice. I didn't give it much thought, though, because I was too busy wondering if I'd survive the night.

Oz had paused the DVR at least three times so I could run downstairs to check on Mom. Her breathing hadn't changed, and she didn't seem to be in any obvious discomfort, and most importantly, she was still alive. A voice inside— the sane voice—said that I was a very sick girl. In logical tones, it reminded me that I was overstressed and that the only acceptable explanation was that I had imagined the events of the last two nights, but the voice of fear told me that something inside me was shifting, changing, and it wasn't just a mental illness. Smells were thicker, intuition— stronger. I even felt physically different. Sure, my entire world was crashing down, but my normally clumsy steps were more sure-footed, and maybe even a tad graceful. The fearful part of me told me that all of this was real, and I was totally and utterly alone. I worried about Mom, and not just because she was on her deathbed. I worried that the thing outside my window would somehow make it in and finish her off. Imagining the monster looming over her still, lifeless form was enough to make me dash into the bathroom next to her room and vomit. I heard Aunt Mag puttering around in the next room and figured she was doing some last-minute chores before turning in for the night.

I was buckling under the new pressures. Life was hard before, but the new problems I'd picked up were beyond anything I could have imagined. And I needed her. One minute later I was bounding back up the stairs and grabbing Oz's hand. "Get your shoes on, we're going on a little trip."

Oz eyed me cautiously, blond hair falling into his eyes.

51

"Um, won't your aunt mind?"

I put my hands on my hips, tilting my head back and making a sound of exasperation. "In case you haven't noticed, I'm of age now. No matter what she says, I'm going."

"But... Wren, don't you think you should kinda stick close to home just in case...you know?" His voice drifted off and he looked away, unable to finish the thought.

A lump gathered in my throat and I stared at him, my chin firming up with the effort it took not to curl up into a ball and cry for my mommy.

"You...you just don't understand." God, that sounded utterly lame and totally typical, and I wanted to smack him for being there to witness it.

He took my shoulders, mouth turning down at the corners. "Uh...Wren, I think I sort of do."

God, how could I forget? Oz had lost his mother at the age of seven to cancer as well. Not a brain tumor, but breast cancer. His father barely kept a roof over Oz's head now, and was an alcoholic. Not the raging beat-you-with-his-belt kind of drunk but the funny, loose kind of drunk who chugs beer at baseball games and laughs in that loud, guffaw kind of way that jolly drunks do. I sort of liked him, even if he was a boozer always one hangover away from getting fired from his job, but Oz resented him with more passion than love could ever instill.

I stepped into his arms. He ruffled my hair, his attempt at turning a weird, sentimental moment into something not so serious.

"Shit," I said.

"Yeah," he agreed.

How could I tell him that I wanted to leave so I could draw the ugly thing that had tried to break into my room away from my home and away from my family? He'd never believe me. I mean, how could he?

"All right, dude. I'll stay, but I'm gonna catch some shut-eye. Come see me tomorrow?" I tried to sound hopeful, relaxed, and didn't think for a second he believed me. Oz knew me better than I knew myself. But he let me think he didn't know better. He shrugged and nodded, and left after he'd told me goodnight.

Sighing, I told my feet to head for the door, but instead I curled up on the mattress, eyes trained on the window, waiting for my doom as my teeth chattered and my bladder protested. Downstairs, my mother lay helpless, head swollen with the thing inside that the doctors wouldn't touch. I wanted to run downstairs and curl up at her side in the small hospital bed, but I wouldn't risk her safety if the thing came back for me.

Maybe I was going crazy, but some spinning, growing thing inside me said otherwise. I felt like a savage wild thing lay waiting, lounging just below the surface. Tonight it had risen to rattle its cage, almost breaking the bars, but I'd held it back. Maybe it was insanity, maybe I was schizo, but it felt like it was more than that.

* * * *

I knew my tormenter waited outside, ready to crawl up the side of the building with his suction-cup fingers and break the glass of my window with one meaty green fist. But even as I thought it, I felt myself drifting down. I jolted awake long enough to run downstairs, grab a carving knife from one of the kitchen drawers, and dash back up to my bedroom. I also turned on the nightlight I hadn't used since I was twelve, and as stupid as it seemed, it gave me a small amount of comfort. I knew the ugly beast was still outside, waiting, grinning and twirling in its tattered clothes, because even though it sounded crazy, I could swear that I smelled it. It smelled like brimstone, sulfur and something that had been left to rot on a sunny roadside for far too long. Eventually, somehow, I slept, and when I woke it was to the screams of my aunt.

Chapter Five

Desperation

Golden, soft sunlight drifted into my mother's chic bedroom-turned-sickroom. A doctor examined her, someone I'd never seen before who claimed to be taking over for Dr. Smoot during his vacation. He insisted we call him Sam, which didn't sit too well with me. Bleary-eyed and with thick white brows that seemed to stay risen in an expression of surprise, he regarded me with sympathy and what almost resembled impatience.

"You'd be doing her a kindness. What you see now is just a body, not the person she once was. The ventilator will keep her heart beating, but the brain..."

"Shut up!" I tried to scream, but it was muffled by my aunt's bosom as I quietly sobbed. I couldn't look at Mom, not with her fingers twitching and her toes occasionally curling spasmodically. Nerves, he'd said it was. Involuntary movements, little neurons firing off in a dying brain.

Aunt Mag was crying too, but managed to keep herself composed. "Dr...uh...Sam. Can I speak with you, privately?"

I was pushing away in a second. "No! No, you will not speak with him privately! I'm her daughter, and I know what that means. I'm eighteen now! I'm an adult. I'm the next of kin. This is my call. Say what you need to say right here. But it doesn't matter what you think. I'm the one who will make decisions over...this. And no! You will not just let her die." I was shaking now, my fists balled up, and I was prepared to kick and scream if necessary. I stomped over to

54

my mom's bedside, looking at her blue-tinged eyelids, and I took her cool, thin hand.

"You'll send the stuff, hook her up, help her breathe... I....I can't accept this. Not yet. No, no, not yet."

"But..." The doctor was getting flustered. Aunt Mag wailed and stumbled from the room with her face in her hands.

"You'll do it, damn it. She's got great insurance, and I know it'll cover the cost. You call them right now." I turned on him, feeling a weird warmth run from the nape of my neck to my toes. I felt the strange, rumbling vibration in my chest again, and suddenly my vision became clearer, more vivid. I smelled his breakfast — bagel and cream cheese, orange juice, cigarettes. I grabbed for the railing of the hospital bed, thinking that maybe I was ready to faint, that I was having a stroke, that I was dying too, but instead I felt strength, strength and more of the rage that for a moment diminished the fear and agony. The room now felt much too small, and I took a deep, steadying breath.

The doctor had gone ashen. He was already pale but I swear, the man gave the white linen sheet my mother lay twitching on a run for its money.

"You just...your face...it..." He fished a hanky from the front of his lab coat, dabbed at his forehead. He turned but kept his eyes on me. "For a second...you..."

I didn't give a flying shit what he thought about my face. Time was running out, and something had to be done. "Call them, doctor. You go out and use the phone in the kitchen. We don't get cell service out here. You tell them to hurry."

"Y-yes, I-I'll call someone right away. M-my condolences." Then he was out the door in a flash. No more adults. Just me, my mildly seizing mother and the potted cactus on her windowsill.

The second the heavy oak door clicked shut, the strength I'd felt just seconds before drained away as if from a hole in a balloon. I plopped down onto the aged, threadbare rug she loved — a gift from her great-grandmother before she'd

55

died of old age—and cried.

* * * *

I oversaw the nurses while they hooked her up to the life support system, turning my head as they shoved the tube down her throat. She'd scared me once, her chest making a rattling, wet noise. She'd stopped breathing for a full minute and I'd panicked, which had made Aunt Mag panic, which had resulted in us both screaming and crying and running around the room as if we could find some magic item that could make her start breathing again. It hadn't occurred to either of us that good ole CPR might have been the best option. But Mom had started breathing again, and the nurses had arrived not even five minutes later.

As the machine began breathing for her I nearly cried with relief. I noticed that her head was more swollen than it had been mere days before and I knew I wasn't doing the right thing. I was keeping her around out of selfishness. I couldn't bring myself to let her go, and even if I knew the woman who had lovingly raised me was probably gone already to the other side, it was still the body that I was used to seeing bustling about the house, or rushing out of the door at three a.m. when a call came through that she was needed at the hospital.

It wasn't our hospital's usual policy to make home visits and bring such equipment to personal residences, but Mom had once been their colleague and everyone had adored her. She shone light wherever she went, and everyone was missing her warmth.

We'd gone to church until she'd gotten so ill she couldn't leave the house without experiencing blinding headaches and moments of intense confusion, not to mention pain. Heaven. Was she already there? I didn't know.

* * * *

I thanked the nurses afterward and left without looking at

56

Aunt Mag, who regarded me with a mixture of pity, apathy and resentment.

"I'm taking Mom's car," I informed her.

"But…you're upset right now, and I don't think—"

"Please, Aunt Mag. I need to get out of here for a while." I turned on her, my back straight, trying to be the adult I claimed to be.

She sighed, fetched the keys from my mother's purse, and told me to drive carefully.

Five minutes later I was pulling into the trailer court with Mom's dark-blue 2010 Beetle. I parked in front of the oldest one and bopped the horn twice. The rickety door swung open and an unshaven face poked around it. Oily brown hair was plastered to one side of his face as if he'd been asleep.

Oz's dad gave me his best smile, the one he'd probably used as a teen when he'd been a popular basketball player, before he was a heavy drinker.

"Hey, Wren! How's your mama? Prettiest lady in Perry County, I always say. Smart, too." He realized his drunken error too late and his face crumpled in such a way that I felt bad for him. "Aw, Wren. I'm sorry. I keep forgetting, you know? It just don't seem real. Just don't seem right."

I smiled out of the Beetle's window, letting him know he hadn't offended. "It's all right, Dave. I forget myself sometimes. She's…in bad shape. The doctors say she isn't going to be with us much longer."

Dave looked down sheepishly and reminded me so much of Oz for a second that my heart squeezed.

"Is Oz around, Dave?" I asked, changing the subject.

"Think so. Just a second. I'll holler for 'em."

Dave bellowed loud enough to startle half his neighbors, informing Oz that his *girlfriend* was waiting outside. Once again, I didn't correct him. It was pretty amazing that Dave could stand upright half of the time, so getting his facts jumbled was just a given. A few minutes later Oz stepped out, shrugging off his father's hand on his back as he told him to go *have fun with his little woman*. I could see a flash of hurt cross Dave's face before he stumbled back in.

Oz jumped into the passenger side. "Was just about ready to head your way. Let's get out of here, huh?"

I nodded, shifting the Beetle into reverse and driving out of the rundown trailer court.

Fifteen minutes later and we were walking down the streets of downtown Hazard. We were in Deno's Dairy Bar drinking strawberry shakes and making small talk about the weather, movies, anything but the obvious.

After we'd finished the shakes and paid for our food, Oz looked up from his texting, tossing his head to get the pretty, spun-gold hair out of his big puppy-dog brown eyes. He caught his tongue ring between his teeth and tapped the table with his fingertips.

"We need to talk," he told me, his eyes darting back and forth then finally coming to rest on my face.

I sighed, standing and shoving my phone into my jeans. "We've already talked about all of this. Mom's on a ventilator now."

He squinted as if the words had physically wounded him. "That really sucks, Wren."

"Yeah," I agreed, gesturing toward the door of the dairy bar. Some old lady at a table to the side was staring at Oz with disapproval, so I stuck my tongue out at her and wiggled it, winking suggestively. Her mouth widened into an O of surprise and one wrinkled hand fluttered to her chest.

"Stop that. She'll tell everyone you made a pass at her. I don't care, really," Oz told me, standing and stretching his back.

I shrugged and pushed the door open, glaring at the old bat before I sauntered out.

We visited the small park in the middle of the city, which consisted of a few benches, some pretty flower bushes and an old, chipped fountain that sometimes didn't work, but was charming anyway. We were alone.

Occasionally a car would pass on the street, or some giggling teens would swagger by the entrance, but no one paid us any attention.

Oz took a deep breath, leaning back with his long, gangly legs spread relaxed before him. His black, buckled boots bounced and wiggled, a sign of impatience, I knew. Or nerves.

"Get it out, already." I sighed, tying my hair back as the sun caused sweat to pop out under my yellow tee.

Oz looked at me, picked at his pierced brow, and obeyed, "Last night, when you asked me to come to the window..."

I sat a little straighter, my heart beating faster, and turned my head and met his eyes. "Yeah?"

"Well, you looked, I don't know, different for a second."

I held my breath, remembering the doctor's comments that morning when he'd been alone with me in the room while I demanded he rush someone to hook my mother up to the ventilator.

He shifted awkwardly in his seat, sitting upright, putting his elbows on his knees and running his hands through his blond hair as it fell forward.

"Um. Yeah. Your face looked a little, I don't know...off? I mean, your expression, it was...not you."

Time had stopped and I felt myself reach out and grab his wrist. "Oz?"

He shook his head, standing up and shoving his hands into the pockets of his frayed, baggy jeans. "Probably just the lighting playing tricks. It was kinda dark in there. I guess maybe you're not the only one seeing shit. Maybe you just had gas."

I shivered, remembering the weird rumble that had begun in my chest on two different occasions—three if you counted my weird nightmares at the old lady's house, which I wasn't even sure existed at this point. I mean, if someone had found me delirious and alone out in the middle of nowhere, why hadn't they called the police? Why hadn't they called an ambulance? Why would they drag me to their grandma's house and let me thrash all through the night? Nothing made sense.

And that was when I made up my mind. I had to go back. I had to find the house I'd woken up in two nights ago. I needed to ask questions. I reached up, felt my neck, but no longer felt smooth scarring. The skin was unblemished and smooth beneath my fingertips. Strange, how I'd dismissed the weird scarring so quickly, but things had been happening so fast I hadn't had a chance to dwell on any particular event.

Then I saw it.

Standing across the street by an old parking meter, a man-shaped shadow hulked. It flickered in and out, the sunlight failing to illuminate the form. Its head was cocked, and though it was faceless, I could feel it looking straight at me. I glanced up, and noticed Oz watching me again. I put my palms on the cement bench, gripping the stone with my fingertips. I looked back at the thing, but it hadn't moved an inch. The shadow flickered again, like a bulb about to blow a fuse. I felt the weird rumble in my chest as warmth bloomed in my stomach, spreading outward into my legs.

"You're doing it again, Wren. I don't like that look..."

But I wasn't listening to Oz. I was listening to something that felt ancient and natural. Something primitive was waking inside, stretching its veiny legs, clawing at my soul and urging me to...

Run, Attack, Bite, Bite, Bite. Make it gone. Destroy it. Banish it.

I rose to my feet and watched as a small, pigtailed girl of about six and her parents strolled toward the shadow across the street. I almost called out, but stood where I was, shushing Oz when he asked what I was doing. The woman walked right through it, not missing a beat, but her animated chatter paused and she shivered as if shaking off a bug.

Then it was gone. The war-hungry thing inside me sighed, curled back into whatever part of my soul it used as its resting place, and went back to sleep.

I took a deep breath, the summer breeze tossing a thick lock of hair into my eyes. I was turning to Oz when I felt something whisper against my jeans—it was a copy of the *Hazard Times*. I picked it up, my heart chilling at the headline.

Three People Missing

I scanned the first few paragraphs, ignoring Oz as he tugged at my arm. Police had no leads, but three people had gone missing in one night, each living several miles apart. One male, two females, all three somewhere in their late twenties or early thirties. Locals had also been complaining of maimed and missing animals, and citizens feared that all of it was somehow related. A cult? A ritualistic serial killer? The boogeyman?

I grabbed Oz's arm, handing him the paper with trembling hands. "You heard of this?"

He looked at the paper, nodded, then sighed, "Yeah. The trailer court is kind of in an uproar. All kinds of rumors going about. Neighbor's dog went missing. Someone's cat, too. Soon as the paper came this morning everyone was calling their neighbors, so they're all paranoid. Might just be coincidence though. The critters might come back. All of this happened last night. Police think it's some kinda cult. But really, a cult? In Perry County? But yeah, just in case, I'd rather you not go out after dark. Honestly though, all of that kinda pales in comparison to what just happened. You did it again. What the fuck, Wren?"

I dropped my eyes to his Weezer tee, taking a gulp of air. The warm breeze suddenly felt frigid and I hugged myself. Oz laid his hand on my shoulder, squeezing gently.

"Wren? Talk to me. I'm starting to freak out a little."

I met his teddy bear eyes. "I don't know. But I think it's all connected. I'm seeing…things, and something is happening to me when I see them. I feel…strange, like

61

there's something inside that's taking over, something... something not human. Yeah, I think we'd better talk."

I checked in with Aunt Mag on the cell, and she informed me that there had been no changes in Mom's condition. I plopped back onto the bench, told Oz to keep an open mind, and started at the beginning.

* * * *

"We gotta find this freak. We gotta ask questions." Oz was pacing. I had to give him credit, he'd stayed quiet throughout the entire thing, but now he was crackling with energy, his sinewy shoulders bunched up with nervousness.

"I'm not even sure it really happened at all. I don't even have a wound, see?" I tilted my neck and he leaned close to inspect. He shook his head, taking my hand and dragging me into the street.

"I don't care. I have no idea what's happening, and we both may be crazy, but I'm not taking a chance. You're taking me to the place and we're going to get answers, now." He met my eyes, catching his tongue ring between his teeth and gnawing on it. I hated it when he did that.

"I can't. I mean, I know where it is, but I can't just walk up and demand their attention. If it really happened, I threw the favor in their faces. I jumped out of their window, for God's sake. And what if something happens? I can't leave Mom for that long. She...she doesn't have long, Oz. You know that."

"Give me directions. I'm driving, just in case you, ya know, spazz or whatever."

I socked him in the arm but he only shook his head, pulling a piece of gum out of his pocket as I gave him girl-directions to the weird old lady's home. He was staring at me as a fat, balding guy in a tie walked by, half tugging his golden retriever behind him. I vaguely recognized him and thought that maybe he was a lawyer. I think he'd spoken to Mom once at the supermarket and had mentioned his firm.

He spoke on a cell phone, his face contorted with anger. Sweat dampened his armpits, and I smelled his rancid odor before he even passed. The golden, long-haired beauty at his heels cowered along the sidewalk, hesitatingly wagging his tail as I made a soft clicking sound with my tongue to let him know I saw him. I scratched him behind the ear as he went past, telling him what a pretty boy he was, and that's when everything went wrong.

I froze, looking down, but instead of my pink-and-black sneakers I saw one yellow, fuzzy paw. Black nails tapped the pavement as I trembled, and smells assaulted me from every direction. An ambulance screamed, shrill and torturous somewhere in the distance, and a sea of voices turned into a jumbled chorus in hell. I could hear Oz's among them, shouting, and I smelled him. Panic, sweat and fear billowed from him in fragrant sheets. I backed up, stumbling as I realized I was on all fours, and in my confusion began a sort of erratic half run. Something landed on me, crushing me to the pavement, and I smelled Oz all around me. "No, not the street. Wren! This isn't really happening, this isn't really happening. No, no, no! Wren, it can't be. No. Don't fight me. Please. Oh God."

His grunt was like a jet engine inside my head as he lifted me into his arms. People stared wildly as he jogged the few feet to my car, opened the passenger side and shoved me in. I landed awkwardly, curled into a ball and regarded my bent hind legs with horror. Golden fur covered what used to be my hands, but was now, very clearly, a paw. I glanced up and saw in the tiny vanity mirror of the flipped-down visor the face of a *dog*. A dog with aquamarine eyes.

The driver's side was flung open and Oz plowed in, shaking and holding his hair back from his face.

"I saw it. I saw what happened...you pet that dog, that dog on the leash. I was looking right at you. I know this is you. I know it... You just melted into...into that." He pointed at me wildly, his finger making jerky circles in the air, and he sounded so loud that I tried to cover my ears, but I couldn't find them on my head. They weren't in the right spot.

My mouth felt long and super, super wet. My nose felt chilly and damp. My body trembled, over and over and over, then Oz was lifting my head from the seat with both his hands.

"Your eyes—they're the same, that same gorgeous aqua color. That's how I know it's you, Wren. That's how I know it's you. Oh...my God." His face lit with wonder, and I suddenly wanted to bite him. He said something about finding the people that had done this to me, hit the gas, and stroked my head like I was Man's Best Friend.

"Stay with me, Wren. Don't pass out on me. Stay awake, girl...I mean... Shit." He beat the steering wheel, which sounded like drums. "I hope you don't get carsick."

And that was the last thing I was aware of before I was slapped awake by the meanest old lady in the world.

Chapter Six

Changes

My eyes flew open and I whined deep in my throat. I realized I was still furry, and thrashed around on a brown, ancient-looking couch. The old lady looked as if she might strike me again.

"I told you to stay put that morning, but you slipped out. I knew you'd be back, you little idiot! I know all about ya. You ain't got no idea what you are, do ya?" Her wrinkled, thin upper lip lifted into a sneer and she pushed graying, springy hair away from her damp forehead.

"Now, Pearl, take it easy on her. She's had a rough week." I jerked my head toward the doorway of the tiny living room, noticing tons of small potted plants on every surface and other odd knick-knacks I didn't dwell on.

My attention was on him.

I whined again, jumping to the floor and giving a short bark. I wanted my body back, and the dude in the doorway was like me. It wasn't just the memory of him changing into the giant white wolf that confirmed that, it was an instinct I hadn't possessed before. We were different, but the same.

The old lady was rambling, something about how she knew everything about me and had predicted my appearance before she'd ever laid eyes on me the first time. My floppy ears perked up a little at this, but I kept my eyes on the boy sauntering into the room with an eerie, graceful almost-slink that said he was much more than he appeared to me.

I hadn't seen him in proper lighting, but even from low

on the ground I was stunned out of my nervous bouncing as I looked into his face.

Full lips were quirked at the corner, mocking, dimpling one olive cheek adorably. Hair black as night tumbled to his shoulders in sleek, shining waves that fell against his smooth, strong brow. His strange green eyes with flecks of gold met mine and his tall, lean body bent into a squat in front of me. A round, plain locket dangled loosely around his neck on a thick, sturdy silver chain.

I half wondered how I could see colors, if dogs could only see in black and white, and also marveled at how I still seemed to be, well, me.

"A golden retriever. Really? Demons and vampires want to feast on your entrails and you pick this vessel for protection?" He rolled his eyes, sighing and calling over his shoulder, "She's awake, human."

At that, another form bolted through the door, this one so familiar that I plopped to the floor on my rump in relief. Oz chewed on what looked like a piece of cornbread from one hand, a glass of milk held close to his lips in the other.

I had turned into a dog, and he was eating?

"Wren. You're awake! Trace says he can help you change back. He says you're untrained, but with a little practice, you can morph into whatever animal you want to at will. That's so badass!"

Change me back, change me back, change me back you useless piece of—

My train of thought was interrupted by the old woman's loud, theatrical sigh as she lifted herself from the worn, outdated couch. She picked her way across the tiny living room, rearranging an old painting on the wall of some purple plant and talking to herself as she swept briskly by Oz as if she weren't a day over thirty. Oz gave her space, sticking close to Trace's back, then I noticed something odd about the room, something that was impossible not to notice—the room had no windows. There were four white lamps with little roses painted on the base two illuminating

66

each side of the room, but it didn't ease my fears of being in a strange room with no windows. A chill shivered down my short spine, and I felt my fur rise on end.

I wanted to wake up and realize this was all a dream. In a panic, I began sprinting from one side of the room to the other, my short hairy legs becoming tangled a few times and causing me to stagger into an old floor-model TV that with an antenna on the top that resembled bunny ears. I tried to scream, but it came out as an awkward bark. Oz disappeared for a second and reappeared without the food he'd been munching on. He dropped — looking relaxed — to his knees on the hardwood before me.

"It's okay, Wren. This guy, the one who saved you the other night, he says he can walk you through changing... back. This isn't permanent. It's okay. It's all going to be okay." Oz's voice turned into a soothing whisper, and I awkwardly stumbled toward him, lying flat on the hardwood and snuggling next to his leg with my shaggy head.

"Change her back, man, she's shaking all over. She's scared shitless." Oz spoke as if I wasn't there, as if I were just a dumb animal that had no clue what he was talking about, but still, I stayed close, breathing in something almost intoxicating that had been tickling at the back of my throat since I'd awakened — a scent. The scent of the boy who unsettled me like no one ever had.

Trace sighed, making his long-legged way over to the couch and managed to plop down with grace. "There is no certain way to reverse it. She has to figure that part out on her own. However, I do know that she'll need to be somewhat calm, and will need to envision her human form. If she can't manage it now, eventually — after a few minutes, hours, or days — her human side will demand control, and she'll be back to normal. She has to silence the animal if she wants it now. Call to her dominant beast and order it back into its cage."

Oz stared at him like he'd just set the couch on fire. "Um,

67

right…" He looked down at me, cupping one hand gently under my muzzle. "So…does she, ya know, think like a dog?" Oz actually made a movement as if he were going to cover my ears with his palms and I shook him off, pushing to my shaky, short legs and crawling under an end table at the corner of the room, as far away from the two as I could get.

"What do you think?" Trace replied, his lips quirking up just once. "She can understand you. She retains her usual eyesight and human intellect, but she's rooming with a beast inside her head. She is very much not human." He crossed one long leg over the other, picking a piece of fuzz from his frayed jeans and inspecting his tight snow-white tee. "We knew about her before she even began the shifting process. There are more shifters other than myself and Wren. I know of at least fifty in Perry County alone. Some are private and prefer to live apart from other humans, others are social and mingle with society on a daily basis. But we all have one purpose. We exist for a very special reason."

"And what's that?" Oz asked, looking for the world like a bright-eyed child settling in for a fairy tale as he stretched out his thin legs before him on the floor.

"We are executioners. Demons, vampires, trolls, whatever nasty things that you can imagine. We are the punishment for those who prey on humans or toil with dark arts. A shifter bite is poison to all. Some turn to dust or just vanish, others have a stronger tolerance and can live for a short time after being infected with our magic, but none can survive a bite. Some of us hunt on an as-needed basis killing nasties, some full-time. Then some…we bargain." He smirked on the last words, winking and popping a piece of chewing gum into his mouth.

Oz appeared both delighted and horrified. "So, these attacks, the ones in the paper. You guys know anything about that?" He quirked a brow, keeping his eyes level with Trace's. I noticed that Oz was only able to tolerate the eye contact for a few seconds then looked away. Instinctively I knew this was a sign of weakness, of submissiveness, and it annoyed me.

I shut my eyes, feeling uncomfortably hot, and wished for my human hands so I could knock the golden doggy hair out of my eyes. I managed to lift a paw and awkwardly swipe, but it didn't do the job. Vampires, demons, trolls? *No, thank you.* I pictured myself in my mind's eye. My slight, slim body, standing just at five-feet-four inches, and just short enough to need to crawl up on the kitchen counters to get to the cabinets above my long, chestnut hair falling in reckless waves to the small of my back that were impossible to comb through when wet. I pictured my clear aqua eyes—eyes that had been full of tears too much recently—with blessedly black lashes and brows. My nose, small and upturned, just slightly crooked from breaking it after falling out of a tree at my grandma's house the year she died. I saw my lips—the top one thin in a sharp Cupid's bow, the bottom one full, and usually swollen on weekend nights from the frenzied kisses of strange boys. I pictured my hands, small and pale, with my thin nails chewed down to dull nubs and the tips a telltale black with resin.

And just like that, I felt a change begin. My stomach clutched in some mystical knot and a tingle ran like lightning from the crown of my head to the tips of my doggy toes. Mere seconds later I was making a nude dash for a crocheted blue and white throw that was neatly spread on the back of an old blue recliner.

Trace laughed merrily, Oz blushed furiously and the old lady burst into the room with a hairpin jutting from between her teeth and one hand holding her gray hair tightly in place on the back of her head.

"Well, wonder what the neighbors would think if I had any, and I had winders?" She cackled.

I covered myself to the best of my ability, but was within a quarter inch of showing everything my mama had given me. My bladder was near bursting, and I resisted the urge to cross my legs. The old lady quieted, shaking her head with one hand still holding the bun in place. She shoved the pin in and put her hands on her small, jutting hips.

I broke the silence. "What? Why is everyone looking at me like I'm going to swing around a pole? Get me my damn clothes, Oz!" I snapped.

Oz looked down at his hands as if he'd just been busted looking at a girly mag by his dad and his blush, amazingly, intensified. "I don't know what happened to them... I mean, I think I remember them kinda falling off of you when you were trying to run into the street but I—"

"God! Could this get any more complicated?" I groaned, feeling the rumble in my chest again as my temper surged. "Oh, no."

Then I was falling to the floor with a heavy thump, looking at sleek wide black paws with amazingly sharp claws curving downward on the tips. I looked up, twitching ears that didn't hear as wonderfully as the dog's had, but still heard the world differently—enhanced. Something swished behind me and I curled around, glancing appreciatively at the long black tail that curled as elegantly as a snake before it strikes. I tested its mobility. I licked my new teeth—smooth enameled spikes, the incisors deadly sharp. My back was long and sleek, and as I walked I luxuriated in my shoulders rolling in an almost sensual way. It felt like home.

Oz jumped to his feet, backing toward the door. Trace's face had gone statue-still, his fisted hands being the only indication of the tension that suddenly swelled in the room like a water balloon ready to burst. The old woman hopped, slapping her hands, a toothy grin spreading and her wrinkles turning her face into an intricate maze of lines.

"There she is. That's our tracker, Trace. True form right there. Ain't she a beaut? Haven't seen a panther in quite some time. Lots of folks say they don't exist. Right there's living proof. Oh...isn't she just lovely. Yes, I knew...knew it from the very first dream, she's gonna save this town. Oh, yes, yes she is." The old lady gave a loud, strong whoop and clapped her thin, gnarled hands.

I left the room, not bothering to look behind me. Suddenly I felt powerful, capable and something that felt close to perfection. I was hungry for something without a name. Justice? Vengeance? Blood? I didn't know, but knew that I needed to quench my thirst and exercise the beast I'd been denying. Before I even padded into the bathroom and stood on all fours before the floor-length mirror, I knew that I was stunning. My fur shone like black glass with highlights of blue that almost glowed even in the poor, dull bathroom light. My belly was lighter, almost chocolate in color. My familiar aqua eyes stared back, but they were shaped differently, rounded and tipped up at the outside corners. I purred in pleasure at my own reflection. I opened my mouth, marveling at my sharp teeth, the incisors looking perfectly capable of ripping meat from bone.

I was a vain beast.

The rational side of me said I should be afraid, that I should be horrified, but instead I sauntered back into the living room, the scents of many herbs and warm bodies and baking bread reaching my new and improved nose. It wasn't as intense as the doggy sniffer had been, not as overpowering, and I liked that. Oz was sitting to my left with Trace, biting on his nails as if he were ravenous for dead skin cells. The old woman lounged in the recliner, looking like the picture of satisfaction.

Trace was staring at me, his face betraying nothing. His words were almost a whisper, "Feels like perfection, doesn't it? Like your old skin was just a closet for your organs. Don't get too comfortable, Wren. You need to stay in control."

I lifted a paw, licking it as if I'd done it a million times and swiping at my head, intent on cleaning myself until I shone.

"Wren." It was Oz. "You're...you're pretty amazing. But...Trace and Pearl need to talk to you. There are...things you're meant to do."

I stopped mid-lick, my fur suddenly standing on end.

71

Something was outside. Bad, the gravelly voice inside cautioned. *Destroy it. Bad. Bad. Bad. Wrong.*

I ran through the small house, knocking down the shoe rack by the front door. I began frantically clawing at the wood like an overenthusiastic poodle that needed a potty break badly. I roared, the sound similar to a woman's scream, with grit and hunger and blood on the notes. I could smell it, the thing outside. It smelled like old death and magic.

I was learning that, yeah, magic had a smell. The old woman reeked of it, but in a good way. I had no idea what she was but it wasn't something natural. It wasn't human like Oz. It was rich and sort of reminded me of cinnamon. Cinnamon and fresh earth. But the thing outside smelled kind of like the demon had—like death, but mingled with wildflowers in the spring. It sensed me as well, somehow I knew that. Hostility and territorial pride hit me, messing with my weird new emotions. Then I felt two sets of hands wrapping around my broad, muscled neck. The old woman was chanting in some strange language, crumbling something that smelled like incense and letting it fall onto my nose and into my eyes. I bucked, trying to get to the thing outside, sensing it coming closer. I wanted to sink my fangs into its neck and carry it away from Oz, out into the woods, and suffocate it. I was horrified at these feelings in some far corner of my brain, but my lust to exterminate the evil outside the door overrode any rational thinking.

"Calm down. Damn it! Calm down!" Trace was yelling, "Damn it, Pearl, work faster! I'm gonna have to shift if this goes on much longer!"

My claws sank into the cedar door like it was butter, leaving long splintered trails down its length.

And—once again—my vision was going black.

Where was Oz? Why were they holding me? Didn't they know something horrible lurked beyond the doorway? It was listening, waiting. Didn't Trace sense it too? Didn't his wolf long to rip it into small disgusting pieces?

It's a trap, my human self rationalized in a fearful voice, *they're going to give you to the evil thing, they're going to sacrifice you. Oz will never make it out alive. You're both going to die.*

"Sleep, shifter, sleep, tracker." The old woman purred into my ear, her voice as silky as the fur she stroked with smooth, calming motions.

And sleep I did.

Chapter Seven

Visions

I dreamed of Mom. I stood at her bedside in a wedding dress. I could tell that it was antique, and the stiff, lacy collar itched and made me feel like clearing my throat. I looked behind me, and leading all the way into the kitchen was the long white train. Gauzy and shimmery, it bunched and made a swishing sound as I walked forward. The bodice was torture, and I felt the tight lacings of a corset beneath. Tiny delicate pearls covered the front with large, white ones sewn in a line around my waist. Aunt Mag sang from the kitchen and I heard the unmistakable clang of dishes. The farmhouse was weird in its layout. Adjacent to the living room was the kitchen, on the right side of the kitchen was the doorway to my mother's room. She also had a private bathroom inside to the left of the doorway. It was a sweet spot. I envied her for it. It would have been super convenient for my three-month party spree when the munchies hit. But it was the only bedroom on the lower floor and Mom had insisted she felt more comfortable being close to the entrance. I really think she liked it there because it was easier to hear me sneaking out with boys back when I had a normal, defiant teenage existence. Now I didn't bother to sneak, not with Mom sick and Aunt Mag too stressed and overwhelmed to stop me.

"This little light of mine, I'm gonna let it shiiiiiine," Aunt Mag sang in-between what sounded like the tinkle of silverware.

I turned back around and found Mom watching me.

Her head was no longer swollen, her eyes were clear and intelligent. Her skin was no longer pale and blotchy but pink and creamy with health. Her gold, glossy curls tumbled over elegant shoulders. She ripped the IV out of her arm, the breathing tube, obviously freshly pulled out, glistening with saliva, in the other hand.

Something bumped my leg through the thick, extravagant wedding dress. I looked down into the soulful brown eyes of the stray dog my mom had taken on as her mercy project. His brown, scruffy coat was now black with soot. He shook like he'd just emerged from water and tiny flecks of black, shiny chucks I recognized as coal bounced across the hardwood.

Something was buzzing loudly, like a wasp nest freshly disturbed, and I resisted the urge to cover my ears.

"You have to send him to me, Wren. You still need me. I can hear him, can't you?" She smiled, her sweet dimples showing.

"Who, Mom?" I asked, my voice shaking, my heart full of fear and longing.

"He's already there. You look just like your father. Did I ever tell you that?"

She hadn't, not really. She'd occasionally say I had his eyes, but sometimes she said it like a grudge.

The stray panted at my side, plopping down on the hem of my dress and getting it instantly filthy with coal dust. He whined anxiously, laying his head on his paws and looking up toward my mother.

I swallowed the lump in my throat. "Mommy?"

She rose from the bed in one swift movement. Tiny little fangs dimpled her full lower lip as she smiled at me with that sweet maternal smile. "*Wake up!*" she roared into my face.

I woke to the smell of cheap cologne and boy sweat. I didn't wear a wedding dress anymore, but instead I wore an ugly flower-printed housecoat with a zipper to the chin. Pearl was standing above me, holding a smoking thing that kind of looked like the dried root of some plant.

My head was in Oz's lap and as I rose he pushed his back against the couch. "Whoa. You're back. It's okay."

A rumble began in my chest and I realized I missed my panther form. For decades the big black cats had been rumored to live in the hills of south-eastern Kentucky, but no one had ever gotten concrete proof. The animal inside me stretched, waking again and demanding attention. Something was wrong. The room smelled wrong. I felt the panther rising again and was in the process of giving in to the tingling change when large hands shot out and grabbed the front of the housecoat, shaking me.

"Don't you do it! Put it away, Wren. Now is not the time. Bad shit could happen." Trace stood beside Pearl, who blew on the root, creating more fragrant smoke.

I struggled, felt the animal inside hiss spitefully, and pushed it back down into its dark, primitive cave. I found my voice, but it sounded odd, gravelly and on the verge of non-human.

"What the hell are you doing?"

Her eyes met mine, alert and annoyed. "Cleaning out the negative energy you've brought into my home. It's like a sewage plant in here with your bad energy, girl."

I'd heard enough. I looked around the room, at the potted plants flourishing everywhere. The furniture all looked like something that had been purchased from Goodwill in the seventies. The floor was scuffed but clean. A huge pot-bellied stove I hadn't noticed gave off a soft orange glow in the far right corner beside the doorway.

I grabbed Oz's hand, flinging my other arm out for balance as I rose and nearly taking out a curling, potted vine on the tiny, chipped nightstand beside me.

I yanked him from the brown couch with surprising strength. "We gotta go. Something…something smells bad here. I know that sounds weird, but there's something out there, and it's not exactly friendly."

Oz looked at his feet, his eyes flicking around the room.

We stood beside Trace and Pearl. Trace raked a hand through his jet-black hair, his green eyes glittering with something I couldn't name.

"You can't, Wren. Not now. Someone here needs to talk to you." Trace didn't seem too pleased with the idea.

I ignored him, trying not to stare at his gorgeous face, and began my shoeless stomp from the room, the old housecoat feeling like sandpaper on my skin. At the doorway, I walked right into what felt like a brick wall. I felt my nose gush instantly as I flew backward, managing to reverse headbutt Oz in the lip.

"Shit, you almost ripped out the ring," he complained. "Why did you do that?"

I grabbed my nose, feeling blood soak the housecoat in a warm flow. It hurt like hell but I didn't think it was broken. "What is this?" I said, raising my hand to touch the invisible wall. Warm electricity flowed under the palm of my hand. "What *is* this?" I shouted, beating on it, freaking out.

The rumble was back but I ignored it, whirling on Trace and the old lady. The room had now become ten times creepier.

The old woman walked easily to the recliner, spreading the skirt of her dress like some Victorian lady. "It's a force field. You won't make it through. Go ahead, beat all day. It won't do you a bit of good. Come back and sit a spell. We gotta talk."

I stomped across the room, leaving Oz to stare in wonder at the place where an open doorway should have been. "No. I have to go. My mom is sick, and I don't know what's happening to me, but I want nothing to do with your weird, hocus-pocus cult stuff."

Trace laughed to my right, lifting a potted plant to his nose—some wide yellow bloom—and sniffing it almost delicately. "Just sit down." He sighed, running his hand on his frayed jeans after he set the plant back down on its small wrought-iron pedestal. "Aren't you curious about what you are?"

"I don't have time," I said, pushing hair out of my face. "My mom could already be dead."

The old woman glared. "Just a few minutes. All I ask of ya."

I gave up, letting my shoulders slump, and tossed myself onto the old, brown couch. After Oz had settled in beside me, wide-eyed, she began.

"Your daddy was a powerful shifter," she sighed.

"What? You knew my dad?" My mouth dropped open.

"Yup. Fine man. Didn't stick around too long. Said he was just passing through. Wasn't aware he courted your mother, but you gotta be his. Only panther I ever heard of in these parts, and you got his eyes."

I stiffened, more curious than I liked to admit. As I processed what I'd been told I was suddenly really, really ticked off. "So he basically knocked my mom up with his demon seed then split?" I met her eyes, and I felt Oz's warm hand slip into mine, squeezing, assuring.

"If that's the crude way you wanna tell it, I guess so. Just up and left one day. Nobody saw him departin' but we all just assumed he'd just moved on to his next town. Drifter, he was. Helped kill a few trolls, a couple of demons. Fierce in his true form."

I cringed. "Demons? Trolls?" I didn't mention the terrible entities I'd seen lately.

"Sorta like the things you've been seeing lately. They're feeling you out. Seeing if you realize what you are. They know there's somethin' special about you, and they wanna know what that is."

I shivered, trying to keep an open mind but wanting to keep it shut if it meant that I had to believe in all of the craziness.

"Did my mom know?" I asked, hearing the accusing tone of my voice.

Her answer allowed me to breathe a sigh of relief. "Don't reckon she did. It's an unspoken rule, we don't talk about these types of things to the blind."

"The blind?" I asked.

She nodded, gesturing toward Oz. "Like this one here before today. Most folks don't know there's otherworldly beings out there, terrible things. Things that can make you go crazy just by lookin' at 'em. They're fortunate. Fortunate and easy prey, especially right now. We got a nest of rogue vampires somewhere, and they're getting braver every day."

She leaned forward, one hand clutching her thin knee through the threadbare fabric of her cotton gown. "You're a shifter. Your kind has been around since almost the beginning of man. No one knows your true origins, but one thing is certain—you were put here by the good Lord to clean up the earth."

"Whoa," Oz marveled at my side. I darted a quick look at Trace, who was standing with his muscled, capable arms folded across his chest. He winked. I looked away.

While I'd been covered in golden doggie fur, I'd heard Trace tell Oz that there were at least fifty shifters in Perry County alone.

"Your bite is the only thing that's deadly to every being. It makes demons vanish, vampires explode and trolls and Fae melt. The calling you feel when you're in true form. It's your destiny."

"True form?" I asked, wondering what the heck that meant.

"Yup," she chirped. "You can turn into any type of creature so long as you got contact with, say, its bones or fur. Even a scale will do. But your true form is the panther, just like Trace belongs to the wolf."

I didn't like the sound of any of it. I could turn into anything I wanted? Any creature I could imagine, as long as I was in contact with some part of it? I wanted to run.

The old lady leaned back again. "This type o' thing would be better taken over a series of weeks, but you get the shock treatment. We ain't got time to be vague. There's a group of rogue vampires dwelling in Perry County. One of our

79

connections claims that they're planning to slaughter the town after they get a few more volunteers. We need all the help we can get."

I held up my hands and cringed at the sight of the ugly flower print on my sleeve. "Uh, no. Not interested. If shit is gonna go down I don't want front row seats. I'm leaving. I'm going back to my mom, and I'm gonna learn how to fight this. I refuse to be a freak."

I stood, turning to ask the question that had been nagging at me since she'd started the conversation.

"What are you?" I asked, squinting.

She grinned, tilting her head, eyes sparkling with mischief that was much younger than her features. "Why, just an old witch."

I shook my head, turning my attention to the invisible door to give it a solid kick. I was getting out of that house and stepping back into the sane, rational world I knew. Screw demons and vampires, and the fact that I could sprout hair in places I would have thought impossible mere hours ago. I was leaving.

"Nothing makes sense. I don't want this. Thanks for the info, but I can't do this anymore. It's time for me to go."

And that's when he walked in. Impossibly tall, he bent as he walked through the force field as if it were nothing. Red, blazing eyes—matching his short, flame-colored buzz-cut hair almost perfectly—snapped to my face with eerie quickness. He looked maybe twenty-one. No older than mid-twenties. I say he looked at least twenty-one not because any hint of age showed on his smooth, pale skin, but because of the way he carried himself. He somehow managed to make walking into the old, rustic cabin look like he was entering a royal ball. He was dressed in a black business suit—it looked expensive. He adjusted his black tie, bowed at the waist, and offered his hand.

"You must be Wren." His face dimpled sweetly as he smiled, close-mouthed. "My name is Laylian. I'm a... business associate of your friends here." His eyes never left my own. The newly awakened part of me felt challenged by this, and the rumble in my chest began to vibrate, working its way into my throat. He looked away, somehow realizing his error, but it was too late.

The beast inside me jolted, clawed at my control, and roared. I wanted to rip into his smooth, outstretched hand with my teeth. His stink hung like mist in the air, death and wildflowers, with faint notes that smelled sort of like cotton candy. I was leaping for him before I knew what I was doing, feeling my body prepare to shift—ready to exterminate my natural-born enemy. My personal fears and human emotions began to shut down and the black panther dwelling in the wild place nestled somewhere in my soul I hadn't known existed before tonight crouched in preparation, licking its chops.

Then Trace was slamming into my side. The growl in my throat turned into an *oomph* as I hit hardwood. He rolled me over, lightning quick, and straddled me, pinning me to the floor. With one free hand he shook me until my teeth rattled. He swatted at someone who landed on his back, and I saw Oz's enraged, shocked face as he flew backward.

The beast inside quieted for a second, whimpering in the face of Trace's dominance. "Don't be a fool! He's not the enemy here! Stop this!" Trace's lips were inches from mine and his breath smelled like spearmint and something else— Pepsi? Wolves drank Pepsi?

The red-haired man in the doorway laughed, slender, needle-like incisors showing beneath his lips. He took out a handkerchief, bending at my side with his knobby knees showing through the fabric of his suit. "I know my presence irks you, but I mean you no harm."

An inhuman scream tore from my throat, my rage so strong that I thought I might choke on it.

Trace held my wrists with one hand, taking the hanky from the red-haired vampire and pressing it into my tense, balled fist. The minute the soft cotton touched my flesh, it triggered one of the most terrifying experiences of my life.

81

Chapter Eight

Paint the Town Red

Images assaulted me – a man with hair the color of fresh snow clapped and roared with laughter. Dingy bulbs hung, all connected with cords that ran the length of an earthen tunnel, illuminating his features. His chin almost came to an actual point, and his nose was much the same. Red eyes, framed with snow-white lashes, blazed hungrily. His lips were thin red slashes in his pale face. His skin was smooth, poreless, aside from a thick pink scar that ran from one corner of his lips to his earlobe. He wasn't easy on the eyes. In every expression, every movement, evil shifted all about his thin, poorly dressed form.

He reminded me of a rat my mom had indulged me in when I was five. She'd read that they made fantastic pets for small children and were surprisingly intelligent. I remembered opening the blue, ribboned box with little air holes poked in the top and squealing with delight when I'd glimpsed my new pet. Inside a large white rat had sniffed at the air, lifting on his hind legs, tiny, pink paws curled against his furry chest. Wide Dumbo ears had twitched adorably and I'd reached in, my hands shaking with excitement. Mom had been smiling, taking out a disposable camera and blinding me momentarily with the flash to capture the timeless, five-year-old birthday memory. I'd lifted him slowly with both hands, stretching out my fingers and quirking my head to the side. "I will name you Kitty," I'd told him, and Mom had exploded into laughter. The loud noise had startled the previously docile, curious creature, and he'd bitten into the padding of my right thumb, hard.

But this creature didn't only bite when startled, out of self-

82

defense. Unlike the white-haired vampire, the rat hadn't had any evil intent buzzing around the tiny brain between his pink, wide ears. He'd drawn my blood out of fear I instinctively knew the monster I now watched in the tunnel would bite for fun.

I suddenly knew that this creature would kill me just for daring to be in his presence, and I tried to float away, tried to find my way back into the warm, unfamiliar cabin I'd found myself in twice without any remembrance of how I'd gotten there. The creature wore, of all things, red sweats and a matching sweatshirt, both blackened with what looked like soot and showing more than a few holes. He lifted a wineglass to his lips, chipped on the edge and full of bright, thick red liquid.

I was invisible, zooming in as an unwilling passenger without control. I wanted far away from the white-haired man and willed the vision to zoom in on something else, someone else – anything but the soulless thing with fangs that elongated every time he sipped the red liquid.

Maybe thirty more crowded around, some well-dressed, others looking like homeless junkies, but all of them covered in the same black grime. A punch bowl sat on an old, rickety foldout table someone had dragged into the bumpy, earthen tunnel. Wide, shedding logs ran from the floor to the ceiling. One of them was beginning to splinter. The area made me feel claustrophobic. A red-eyed man wearing Hawaiian shorts and a wife-beater passed out drinks, all of them the same thing the white-haired vampire was drinking from his chipped wineglass.

In the laughing, pressing mix of grimy bodies I saw three limp forms piled next to the table. One of the women had been blonde, and managed to look pretty even covered in black dust with her hair falling in soft waves around her oval, clear face.

The other woman was portly, with chubby white hands with fingers that looked raw and chunky on the ends. She had one eye open, but thankfully she'd never see the horrible, disgusting scene unfolding before her.

The man was shirtless and his bird-like arms were locked in a frozen embrace with the chubby woman whom, I thought sadly, had a sweet face. The man's hairline was receded, but his wide,

83

brown eyes would have been lovely had they not been glued in the telltale stare of a traumatic death.

All three had something in common, aside from being dead, that is. All of them had jagged, open gashes for throats. Suddenly I knew what they were drinking from the bowl on the table. A squabble broke out among two over a glass, their eyes blazing red and their fangs bared at one another. The taller one in a blue T-shirt with a backward black hat grabbed the smaller vampire by the throat. The smaller one looked sixteen at most, with boyish, chubby cheeks and freckles spreading over his flat, wide nose.

Backward Hat looked older and his rat-like features became sharper as he sank his fangs into the smaller vampire's cheek. Meat ripped away and the vision zoomed in for a close-up.

The white-haired vampire was there in a second, grabbing both by the neck and lifting them in each hand until their feet dangled from the ground. With a grin, he knocked their heads together, blood spraying the crowd. The two fell, still moving and trying to claw at each other, even with pulp for faces. The crowd cheered, raising their glasses.

My eyes snapped open and I rolled over, puking onto the hardwood. I tossed the handkerchief away, wiping my mouth and struggling to push Trace off of my body.

"What did you do to her?" It was Oz, screaming. The old lady stood beside him, her small, bony hand gripping his forearm, her knuckles white with the force of holding him back.

Laylian wasn't smiling anymore. Trace pushed himself to his feet, freeing me of his weight, and I rolled to my left, trying to put as much distance between myself and the red-haired monster as possible.

"Don't...don't touch me," I managed weakly, a sob breaking from my chest and tears dripping onto my fisted hand. "Oh God," I wailed, wanting to go home and never come near the cabin again. I wanted my mom. I wanted her more than ever. If she were conscious, she'd know what to do. It wouldn't have gone so far if she were here to guide me, to keep the monsters away with that warm, healing

84

light of hers.

Laylian shifted away, obviously trying to make it look as if he gave a damn about my wishes.

"I'm sorry. I imagined it wouldn't be pleasant, but I'm truly sorry this was necessary. There are some of my kind who…do not respect human life. Those are the ones you saw, the criminals of our kind. Animals who do not care about the law. Pearl here told me you had a gift, that she'd seen it in a vision. She said you were a natural-born tracker. We've only known of one other to exist, and she died a long, long time ago."

Something buzzed in my head, and something pulled taut. I retched again and suddenly I knew exactly where the horrible creatures I'd just witnessed feasting on the dead, missing persons were. It was like a psychic trail of breadcrumbs, and suddenly I could see a blue, glowing line flickering, zigzagging through the house and leading to the place where the beasts dined on their savage meal. It was in our town. I'd never actually been inside any of the old abandoned mineshafts, but plenty of the places existed. Most were boarded up or had been collapsed intentionally after the coal had been mined to the best of the miners' ability. Some went on for miles, running underneath the green, rolling mountains that were rich with fossil fuel.

I sensed them all, still, like the lingering feeling of nausea, but worse. I pushed myself up weakly and Oz dashed to my side, helping me stand on my wobbly, numb legs.

The red vampire stepped closer, and Oz stepped in front of me. I grabbed on to the back of his shirt for balance, peeking around his side at the red-eyed, red-haired vampire who seemed downright courtly when compared with the vampires I'd seen in the vision. He was classy, even with his empty, vivid red eyes.

"Stay away from her, man," he told the vampire in a trembling voice, the words sounding far braver than his tone. Not that I could blame him. I was shaking like a leaf, feeling dirty, sickened and more terrified than I'd ever been

85

in my entire life.

"Time to go, Wren," Oz ordered, his voice wavering. He wrapped his arm around the small of my back, holding on to the fabric of the ugly housecat and dragging me toward the door.

Then Pearl was standing in front of me. I jumped, wondering how in the blazing hell she'd managed to get there without my seeing her, or breaking a hip. "My barrier still holds true and you ain't going nowhere. I give you my word that he ain't gonna hurt ya. If we were gonna skin your hide don't you think we would have done that a long time ago, while you were passed out and at your weakest?"

Then she stretched out her steady, liver-spotted hand. I cringed away, digging my nails into Oz's forearm. "Stay away from me, freak! All of you. Stay away from me or I'll…I'll…"

Her hand shot out the rest of the way, her palm resting warm against my cheek. I tried to twist away and she closed her eyes, swaying only slightly. She reminded me of the old ladies in church who stood up to pray, hands raised high in supplication and making you wonder if they're going to collapse into a heap of strong perfume and bobby pins.

And oh God, it felt better than the afterglow of the world's best massage. The beast inside not only quieted, but fell into a deep, contented sleep. I sighed, sagging a little, and Oz's arm tightened around my waist.

"Ma's got ya. Ain't gonna let nothing hurt you. Go, sit back down. You've had a troublin' day. You're tired, Wren."

I nodded, a slow, goofy, sedated grin spreading across my face. "Okay," I breathed. "That sounds nice."

But Oz was pushing forward, walking sideways and regarding the old woman as if she were a rattlesnake with venom-dripping fangs. "Don't touch her anymore. Don't even come near her, or I swear…"

She grabbed his arm, and he gave a squeak. That was the end of our denial of her hospitality.

* * * *

Later, I was sipping on a hot cup of sassafras tea. Little bits of brown floated in the mug, and I nibbled on them absently when I caught one in between my teeth. The sweet, tart liquid had always been a favorite, and I had to admit Pearl's was just as good as what Granny used to make.

"I don't use that ole fake sugar. I get it from an old woman down the street. Grows her own cane. Sweet ole thing, she is. Her sinnin' husband drinks like a fish, plays his banjo on the porch at three a.m. in front of the neighbors and God and everyone. I've heard tale he's been giving that ole slut Millie money for —"

Trace sighed from his place on the floor. He was stretched out like he lounged on the most comfortable mattress in the world, eyes closed, arms folded over his eyes. His shirt had slid up, revealing ripped abs and a line of fine black hair that disappeared beneath his jeans.

I cleared my throat, peering down into my mug as if I could read my future in the bits of sassafras floating there. Oz sat to my right on the loveseat, looking like he was trying really hard to remember something important. Pearl rocked in the recliner, smacking her lips as she sipped her tea and glared down at Trace.

"Mind your manners," she said stiffly, hunching her shoulders a bit and casting a worried glance at the man who dominated the whole couch to my right.

The elegant and abominable Laylian was watching me. His head was tilted to the side like a bird staring into a mirror, motionless, amused, his red eyes twinkling merrily.

I still felt the calming effects of whatever Pearl had done to me, but my heart would speed up occasionally and I would think about Mom, wondering if I'd make it out to see her again before her body finally gave up. I wondered dimly if I'd die here. Maybe Pearl was heating up her oven, maybe sharp knifes were spread out under a cloth on her kitchen table. Maybe she was going to dice us up, toss in some greens, and all three of them would say grace over Wren and Oz stew.

"Wren," Laylian purred. He didn't have any accent I could detect. He didn't have my own slow, easy twang, but he didn't strike me as a city slicker or a foreigner. He could have hailed from anywhere…everywhere. His energy filled the room and the smell of death and the absurd dash of wildflowers and cotton candy was clashing with the sweet licorice smell of the tea.

I met his eyes, those red, blazing eyes, and realized my vision was changing, too. Colors popped, vivid and bright. I could see that his lashes were red as well. A true ginger if ever there was one. He'd removed his tie, holding it in a loosely curled hand. The other rested on his thin knee, and he quickly brushed away a piece of brown fuzz he'd most likely picked up from the couch on the white linen button-up shirt beneath his black blazer.

This time his eye contact didn't strike me as a challenge, now his stare just creeped me out.

I coughed, clearing my throat. "Get on with it."

He smiled. His fangs were smaller now, but I noticed his eyes kept straying to the front of my crusty, bloody housecoat. I would have thought he was staring at my boobs had the ugly, shapeless thing covering me been tighter. His fangs extended, growing larger, and retreated when his eyes once again flicked back to mine. He breathed in deeply, seemed to compose himself, then went on. "I'm sorry if I gave you a fright. You're not a captive here…we just have…certain business matters to discuss."

I waited for him to go on, crossing my legs and shooting Oz a look. He stared at the floor, his mouth working, mumbling without sound. I needed that best friend, shared *oh shit* look to pass between us. I felt alone, and vulnerable, and wished that he'd wake up and reassure me in some way.

Laylian went on, "I live in this area occasionally. I like the layout of the land here. You can hide just about anything

88

in these mountains. But I have many homes—some of them very far away. I know you still must be in a state of shock, and I've been informed that your home life is also in upheaval currently. Normally I would let you come to me willingly, but time is precious. A rogue vampire—Brass, we call him—has put together a small army. They've migrated here from a New York clan and they've gone quite mad."

He paused, sitting upright, and ducked his head just a bit. His eyes blazed at me beneath the fringe of red lashes, and suddenly I couldn't look away. He had my attention, and I felt something inside shift, open and prepare to absorb everything he said.

"We've been informed that his...small army, is preparing to declare war on the humans here. But a war is a mutual thing, so that isn't quite the correct word. They're preparing a slaughter, a message for me, a final slap in the face of our government. Already they've taken three that we know of, and even as we speak, since the sun has vanished, they may be taking more. I need your help. I'm prepared to pay you whatever sum you desire to assist me in finding their den so they can be...punished properly. Shifters are often born with other talents, sometimes one, sometimes many more, and one of yours is the gift of tracking. You know where they're staying, don't you? You could lead us there. Trace will assist in the...punishment for the crimes they've committed. You will not be obligated to assist us in that challenge. All I ask is that you take us there, show us the way."

Insane, inappropriate laughter bubbled past my lips and I lifted the mug of sassafras to my face in an attempt to hide it. "You're a, vampire, right? One of your kind tackled me the other night while I was taking a midnight stroll. He bit me, here." I tilted my head back and ran my hands over the smooth skin that had been weeping gashes just two nights prior. "Crimes, you say? Tell me—what do you live off of? Do you like a fries with your Big Mac? I know what you eat. And oh, don't even bother searching for the three humans you pretend to be concerned about. They're dead. The vampires you're referring to opened their necks and drank their blood from glasses like beer at a frat party."

Beside me, Oz made a disgusted sound, and I smelled the tang of what I now thought was fear once again radiating from him instead of the confused relaxation.

I stood on shaking legs, bent and placed my mug on the floor, and made a grab for Oz's tense hand.

I looked at the vampire. "I won't help you. I don't understand what's happening to me, but I'll figure it out without you guys. I want nothing to do with this…mess. It's your problem, not mine. I have enough shit to deal with at home. Keep your money."

"We don't kill humans. Not normally," he said, as if that statement would make me plop back down on the loveseat and say 'Oh, gee, really? Well, that changes things. Where do I sign?'

He cleared his throat. "We have volunteers. Donors. Humans who actually enjoy being fed from. They're treated humanely. Spoiled, even. We're not as monstrous as you may think. I keep a tight leash on my people. They obey. If we were as savage as you might believe, you humans would have been extinct long ago. There are laws. What is happening here with the deviants is unacceptable, and we would like nothing more than to correct it."

I looked down at Trace, who had turned onto his side, elbow extended, his head propped on the palm of his hand. "It's good money, Wren. And it's for a great cause. It's what we were born to do. I turn ninety this winter, and for seventy of those years I've been helping keep this town safe."

Someone might as well have punched me in the gut. He was ninety years old? From the looks of him he could have been in my graduating senior class. I reeled and Oz stood, shaking his head and looking like he'd just woken from a deep, foggy sleep, and said what I was thinking—

"What the shit, man? You're like, our age."

Trace laughed, lying back down and covering his eyes once more, "Just one of the perks of being a shifter. We don't age, we just—improve."

I didn't want to think about what that meant for me. The room tilted again, and the tea worked its way from my stomach back into my throat. I covered my mouth with my hand, trying to keep from spewing again. The curdled scent of my vomit from earlier still assaulted me, even though Pearl had tackled the mess with towels, a mop and something that smelled like lavender and pine.

"Home, Oz, now." I crossed the room, staying as far away from Laylian as possible. I expected to hit the invisible barrier again, but when I tested it with my hand my fingers only passed through air. Oz was beside me, looking over his shoulder as if expecting someone to sink their fangs into his back.

"I'm prepared to give you your heart's desire!" Laylian called. His voice was no longer smooth and composed. Now, a note that sounded a bit like desperation quivered there. "Anything you could possibly dream of. Name it, and it's yours!"

"Let 'er go, Laylian. Give her time to come to terms. I know we ain't got much to spare, but consider what she's been through. She can't deny what she is forever. Eventually, her panther will win."

I ignored them, and soon we were skidding and braking awkwardly down the steep, rugged rocky road. Oz drove, not saying a word. I stared out of the passenger side window, hugging myself with my arms, sniffling and watching the dark, shadowed trees creep by until we hit the main road. Oz breathed a sigh of relief, rolling his head around to stretch his neck and wincing.

91

Chapter Nine

Floral Secrets

Oz was silent until we were parked in the driveway. He turned off the motor, extinguished the headlights, and stared at me. His pale head stood out against the night and his voice was calm and strangely low.

"Did that really just happen? Am I dreaming, Wren?"

I leaned forward, dug around under the seat and found the sweet spot where I stashed my cigarettes in case of emergencies. "Yeah. Unless it's me that's doing the dreaming."

I lit up, cracking the window, watching the porch light flick on. Aunt Mag would be waiting, and my stomach knotted with dread at the prospect of facing her tonight. My nerves simply couldn't handle another confrontation, and I almost whimpered aloud when I remembered what I was wearing—a blood-splattered, flowered housecoat that could have easily been worn by Granny from *The Waltons*.

"Just kill me now, please." I pushed the cigarette through the crack in the window, and it left a trail of bright orange ash and chemicals as it rolled down the side.

"This...this is like, some wicked Stephen King shit." He cracked the door and the electronic bell chimed frantically.

I'd finally agreed to let him escort me in, on the condition that he do all the talking. As expected, Aunt Mag waited beyond the door with her foot tapping. This time she was wearing gray sweats, her brown hair lying limp and curling around her wide shoulders. She stared down at me, and I felt delicately small, like a twitching-nosed rabbit staring

92

up at the big bad wolf before it gobbles it up in one bite.

Funny how that didn't sound like such an unlikely comparison anymore.

"What...is that?" She sounded tired. Good. That meant her lecturing wouldn't carry her usual fire. I could tell she hadn't drunk her twentieth cup of coffee yet.

Oz took his cue. "Uh. Wren and I were working on our Halloween costumes. I know it's early, but we wanna get really creative this year." God. He was failing so hard that I almost cringed. He even had to look up a bit at Aunt Mag. She was impressive, towering above me and reminding me of a female bouncer. Oz gulped audibly.

"Spare me," she sighed, grabbing the bridge of her nose and wrinkling her forehead. "Wren, you stink. It smells like...blood. What happened?" She didn't sound as horrified as she should have, which said a lot about my behavior these past few months.

"Nosebleed. Aunt Mag...how's Mom?" I tried to keep the exhaustion and fear out of my voice.

Her bleary eyes swept down my figure, her brows coming together as she stepped to the side. "No change—not that I believe you're concerned. Go clean up. There's a casserole in the fridge. The hospice ladies visit again tomorrow, and since you're the one making all of the decisions suddenly, I think you should stick around to oversee everything."

I swept by, head lowered. Oz complimented Aunt Mag's hair sheepishly, remarking that it was getting longer. I checked in on Mom, the machine buzzing and dutifully forcing air into her tired lungs. Guilt squeezed my guts and I told Oz to go hang out in my room for a while.

I shut her bedroom door, listening as Aunt Mag threw something in the microwave in the kitchen, and grabbed Mom's cool, still hand. The doctor had been giving medicine through her IV drip to help with the twitching that disturbed me so badly, and I was grateful.

I almost wished I'd never woken up in the cabin tonight, that I'd stayed asleep like Snow White. Death scared me, but the thought of death touching my mom scared me way more. I was guilty, and part of me wanted to call the doctor, tell him to rush over and give her the peace she'd been denied. But I couldn't. That immature part of me that refused to grow up repeated over and over that if I waited a little longer, something magical would happen and my mom would wake up healthy. The blooming, manically insane part of me whispered that I might possibly be dreaming, and that I might possibly wake up at any moment and find myself back in school, excited about graduation, with my mom bustling about the kitchen and reminding me daily to concentrate on my stack of college applications.

I had failed her — in every single way. I'd thrown away the stack of college applications just last week. I'd fried so many brain cells, the ones that carried ambition, and I couldn't do the one thing I knew she would want me to do — let her go.

"Mom," I said, brushing her fair hair away from her cheek and tucking it behind her ear. "If you can hear me, if you're aware at all, you're probably really mad at me. But…things have been happening, things I didn't think we're possible before. There's…magic. Real magic exists. Dad wasn't what you think he was…he wasn't even really human. Or did you know? Is that why you've never really talked about him? Is that why you never encouraged that I find him? You could have sued him for child support or something, right? But you never did. Did you know, Mom? Did you know that he didn't give you a human child? God, I wish you could answer me."

I lay my head on her hand, knowing that I stank of blood and the weird, smoking root Pearl had waved all around me, claiming that I had brought my bad energy into her home. But it was sort of true, wasn't it? I was bad. I wasn't even human.

"I'm sorry," was all I could say. As if that would fix everything. As if she would suddenly wake up without the bulge in her scalp and forgive me and make all of this right.

Her hand twitched. Twitched, then squeezed. Her fingernails bit into my palm. I looked up and around the tube that breathed for her. Her mouth moved as if she were trying to say something.

"Mom?" I whispered, my heart slamming against my ribcage.

I stood up, ready to run out and grab Aunt Mag. I didn't know why — it wasn't like she could translate — but I needed her to see what I was seeing. The doctor had said she wasn't there anymore. That she wasn't really alive. But my gut told me otherwise. And suddenly I smelled her, and it wasn't the sickbed smell. Her perfume and Dove soap scent filled my nostrils. I wondered if this meant she was dying, really dying. Maybe her spirit was trying to communicate? Comfort me?

"She's not dead," someone spoke, and my butt suddenly felt nailed to the wooden seat we'd dragged from the kitchen to use when we wanted to visit with Mom.

Laylian stood by the window, red hair startling against the white of his skin. His pale hands prodded the dying cactus on the sill, and he was looking at my mother with something that could have been sympathy.

I opened my mouth to scream but in a blur he was on me, one slim, cold finger pressed to my lips. My vision sharpened and I saw his fangs lengthen. My eyes were suddenly a microscope, and I could see that pale pink fluid was dripping from the tiny, hollowed needle tips. I smelled it, too, and it not only smelled like death and rot and magic — it smelled medicinal.

"Don't scream. I'm not here to hurt you, or anyone else. Your aunt has conveniently taken a nap, and will remember eating a hearty ninety-nine cent TV dinner and watching *The Golden Girls*."

The world suddenly seemed more vivid, with thicker smells and a million tiny sounds. I was focused on his finger across my warm, soft lips. I had been wishing that I possessed his speed, his agility, his strength so that I could

95

hand his ass to him and get him out of my home. My scalp tingled, and I prayed that I wouldn't turn into the panther now, not with my aunt so close by, even if the shift was beyond thrilling. But this was different. Then I felt…cold. The panther wasn't growling, it wasn't bashing against the cage of my psyche and demanding I let it free. My eyes went wide and I began to quake, my hands seizing and twitching like Mom had been doing only that morning. I actually felt myself grow taller, my breasts flattening like someone had shoved in a vacuum and turned it on high. Something that shouldn't have been between my legs was magically just *there*. Something chicks don't have. You know when your foot falls asleep and when you stand, that first, icy tingle alerts you before it kicks into that awful, crawling sensation? It was like that.

Laylian's red eyes widened and he backed away, murmuring something that sounded suspiciously like a prayer.

"It's not possible," he breathed, his grace gone as he bumped against my mother's bed with the bends of his knees.

I felt my teeth change and two sharp points poked at my lower lip. The effect was like ice water, and with a final surge of tingling cool pricks at my scalp, I shrank, finally me again.

I found the chair and plopped down, the vampire in the room now not my biggest concern. "Was that what I think it was?" I whispered, not looking up, not wanting to see the scared look in the vampire's eyes that disturbed me more than his creepy, predatory gaze.

"You can only shift into…beasts. Natural things. Not… not…" He was flustered, and his hand went to his hair. "Oh…the value. You could be such an asset. It's miraculous. Pearl didn't mention this. Does Trace know?"

I put my hand in my hands and I felt my chest rumble. I took a deep breath, concentrating on my jeans. On the human things. I pushed the cat down.

96

"Did I...?" I couldn't finish. I didn't want to.

"Yes. For a brief moment I was staring at a mirror image of myself. You shifted...into a vampire. Only the eyes were... different. They were yours."

I pointed toward the window. "I'm assuming you came in that way. Leave. Now. I can't deal with this, not tonight. Do you not fucking see what I'm dealing with right now? Doesn't it strike you as odd that I'm not even really scared of you?"

He composed himself, smoothing the front of his suit and flicking the nail of his index finger against his thumbnail. "You shouldn't be fearful of me. To me, you're poison. It's in your blood, a gift, and although you don't see it as such now, one day you will. I could withstand your bite longer without exploding into dust unlike the majority of my kind, but I would expire eventually. You're powerful...I didn't even realize how powerful. I have known Fae that can take on the likeness of another being, but it's only glamour. They cannot change as you do. With someone like you..."

"Yeah, well, it's not happening. Regardless of what I am, my life is here." I gestured toward my mother's still, pitiful form. "And if...when she goes, I'm gonna hit the road and forget Perry County and everyone in it." I spoke convincingly, and realized with a start that it wasn't just rambling. I hadn't planned on leaving upon my mom's death, but deep down I knew it would be exactly what I would do. "Out," I whispered, still unconvinced that Aunt Mag wasn't awake.

Laylian turned.

"One more thing," I asked. "Did you hurt her? My aunt? Did you bite her?"

"No," he said matter-of-factly. "It's a talent—persuasion."

My chest rumbled again. "Get out, quick. I don't wanna..."

"I'll take my leave." And I believed him. His shoulders had slumped at just the right moment, defeated. Then he said that one word that every teenager despises the most. "But..."

I waited.

"What if your mother could be healed and live even longer than yourself?"

My breath stopped mid-exhale. The beast inside shuddered and I felt it settle in, ears back, hunkered down, waiting.

A strange feeling sparked then, hesitantly beginning to bloom in my chest and worked warmly up into my throat. Suspicion warred with what I suddenly realized was hope, and I could hear both in my voice when I spoke.

"You're just being a bastard. You're messing with me. Why are you doing this?"

I expected him to sneer, to see the sparkle of amusement in those fiery red eyes, but his face remained expressionless. He stepped closer, any hesitancy gone, and in two seconds he was nose to nose with me.

"I may not be a man, but that doesn't mean I'm dishonest. If I wanted, I could have you hauled out of your warm, sad little nest in the dead of night and delivered to my doorstep with a pretty pink bow on top, but instead I'm being a gentleman, and yes, a businessman. One performs much better if they operate on their own free will. I'm being very generous, Wren. I mean to have you on my side, one way or the other. This can be as easy, or as excruciating as you want it to be. I'm offering her clarity, a life without pain, an escape from the casket your aunt ordered last week. Oh, you didn't know that? It's red, with gold trim and embroidered with roses inside. Very quaint."

My heart slammed in my chest and I tasted blood, realizing from far away that I had bitten my lip to keep myself from shattering into a million sobbing pieces. The offer was seductive and my knees grew weak with longing and fear. But I wasn't an idiot. Mom had raised me to know that any deal that sounds too good to be true usually is. There's always a catch, a convenient glitch that's never mentioned during the bargaining. He was being very clear—I could deny him, tell him to get the hell out of my house and be

98

dragged kicking and screaming to his den by God knew what type of creatures, or I could aid him in his quest to exterminate the evil lurking in the abandoned coal mines of Perry County, picking off my neighbors one by one and draining them dry. I would watch my mother slowly die, her fair head swollen and misshapen, and go crazy with grief, or I could give her life and use the animal inside to assist the vampire in her bedroom.

"How?" My voice sounded broken, like a sleepy child. "How…how could you? She's dying. She has a brain tumor. Her kidneys are shutting down, so how? How could it be possible?"

He held my eyes, his own blazing brighter for just a moment, and placed his hands on my shoulders, being careful not to touch any exposed skin. "I would not consider such a thing were you not…so very special. I am offering her the gift of immortality. Help us, and your mother will live forever. I vow to take her under my wing, into my home, and I will see to her happiness. She's a beautiful woman, even now, and would have no trouble blending in to our circles."

I felt like my spine was twisting, and my stomach lurched. I began panting, looking from my mother's still form to Laylian's electric red eyes. Now I knew what he meant, now I knew what he was proposing, and everything in me knew that it was wrong, that it was cruel, that I would be stealing her natural death and forcing her into a world that was wicked, twisted and terrifying. Agony burned in my chest and I grasped at the front of the ugly, soiled housecoat and pressed my palm firmly over my breaking heart, trying to make the ache go away, trying to get more air.

Could I?

Yes.

Because the other part of me was missing her eyes being open, and that part was twirling with excitement and overflowing with hope.

"She would…be like you?" I forced the words out, trying

to look beyond my loneliness and desperation and see the bigger picture. "But then she would—"

He cut me off. "There is no other way. But there are…. donors. She will not be harming humans. She will have more than enough nourishment from the willing."

My blood ran cold. I couldn't bear to think about what he was saying in depth. I tried to push the mental image as far away as I could before I puked on his expensive shoes. I began to tremble. But my mind was bending, my heart was shattering, and grief is the worst emotion you can make decisions with. It makes you desperate. Nothing can make you don a pair of rose-colored glasses quicker than grief, and Laylian knew it. His entire body settled then into another emotion. His face smoothed even further, his red eyes twinkled and his lips turned into a smug, pale pink slash. But right away I didn't recognize the look—deep, relieved satisfaction with a dash of cockiness—I was reeling from the possibilities.

I heard someone talking, questioning, and realized it was me. I hated myself in that moment, I hated the words, but I was powerless to ignore the chance that I might have my mother with me again, moving, walking and talking.

"But…everyone knows. Everyone knows who she is. Everyone knows she's dying. Everyone." My voice was a manic whisper and I muttered more words that even I didn't comprehend. My body was crackling, and I felt like I was floating above myself and witnessing this all from another's vantage point.

His smiled, slender fangs poking out and dimpling his full lower lip, "You just leave that up to me. I'll handle everything."

I sat in the chair for a good five minutes, shivering so hard I cradled myself. My teeth chattered, muscles jerking throughout my body. Adrenaline, hope and horror collided and I felt myself nodding, knowing it was a mistake. Knowing how selfish I was being. Knowing that I would stab a carving knife into my right eye if it meant she'd get

100

better. I would do anything, anything at all if it prevented me from having to lay her in the cold earth. Guilt tried to reason and the beast inside ran nervously in circles, but my head just kept nodding and nodding and nodding, agreeing to let the unnatural thing in my room turn my mother into what he was.

Mom's leg twitched, almost as if she were objecting. I don't remember leaving the room, because my body was humming with energy, my scalp tingling and crawling. I ran through the house, not stopping to check on Aunt Mag or to tell Oz that I was leaving. The big black cat inside purred, satisfied that I was finally losing my tight hold on its leash, fur bristling with pleasure, and I had barely made it over the pavement of the highway and into the field across when I shifted. Shoes I didn't even realize I'd been wearing, old and slightly too big, tumbled into the grass behind me, snagging on one of the nails of my back paw. My last real human thought was that they probably belonged to Pearl as well. My back became long and graceful, my ribs shifting, rippling under my hide. My mouth became larger, elongated, and my teeth were sharp against my lipless mouth.

The panther growled, shook its mighty head, and the rational, sane part of me pulled away, exhausted, and hopelessly watched from somewhere inside—distantly fascinated, and more than willing to give up control. The animal I'd become ran, cutting into the opening forest gracefully, paws lightly thumping on the fertile, damp soil. I inhaled, smelling pine and honeysuckle and…something else.

I stopped, lifting my wet, blunt nose and sniffing the air. Sulfur and death and magic filled my lungs and I shook my large, sleek head. This smelled different from Laylian. It reminded me of old, chunky, spoiled milk. My mouth filled with saliva and my rough tongue tickled at the ribbed roof of it. I wasn't hungry, not exactly, but the beast I'd succumbed to escape my self-disgust and fear was in the

101

throes of desire. A desire to kill.

My long tail swished, and my ears instinctively went flat against my head. I crouched low to the forest floor and began to slink forward. My strong shoulders rolled as I crept carefully through the brush. Then I heard it—something exhaled. The sound was full of anticipation, like the sound you make when you're lifting a spoon of your favorite ice cream to your lips on a hot day.

No more than thirty feet into the valley between two large, looming hillsides sat a rock I'd gotten pretty familiar with on nights when I wanted to toke. It was a rough circle, maybe as wide as your average kitchen table and perhaps three feet in height. Although my eyes were my own, they were enhanced, able to see much better in the dark, which was convenient because it gave me a fine view of the horrible thing crouched upon it.

It had the legs of a deer, and one cloven hoof stamped when it realized I could see it. The rest of its body, aside from the head, was humanoid, but this thing wore no clothing. Pale, puffy skin that reminded me of that of a corpse found floating in the water shone startlingly white in the moonlight. I assumed it was male, if I could judge from the thick black hair in the center of its chest, but between its legs where his junk should be, there was nothing but a smooth, gray triangle of flesh It was growling, and now that I look back, I suppose I would be pretty pissed too if I didn't have any sexual organs. Four gnarled horns curled like dying limbs upon its head, all parallel to one another. What I guess was a nose was composed of nothing more than two wet, dripping holes. The eyes were wide, reminding me on some distant level of an anime character—they had no iris, just large, black circles swimming in the white fishbowls of its lids. The teeth were vaguely human, unless you counted the long, icicle fang that ran from the very center of its upper gum and stopped just past the tip of its pointed chin. Pale, thin lips quivered, and it made a sniffing noise, tilting its head and leaping heavily from the rock onto the forest floor, its hooves sinking deep into the pine needle-covered earth. I smelled feces, anger and sensed its lust for killing, and for a moment, I felt a small, faint tickle of fear. I was crawling toward the surface of my mind, screaming at the black panther to turn with its tail between its legs and run, but I felt my hind legs dig in stubbornly as the newly awakened part of me crouched, ignoring me and pushing me back down into my distant, observant vantage point.

The demon roared then snorted, spittle and thick, black mucus falling to the valley floor and smoking as it touched the grass beneath. Then it was running, its bloated belly jigging as it made its surprisingly sure-footed way toward me.

My vision went red, literally, and I felt electricity shoot through me. I smelled my own tangy magic and as I leaped, I could have sworn that for a moment, I floated. I saw myself ready to land, but in my murderous rage I had misjudged the distance and my own amazing strength. Instead of sinking my fangs into its throat, I sailed over its head, a small stinging sensation blooming on my rear inner limb as I hit the ground behind the roaring horror. I'd been nicked by one of its horns, but I wasn't concerned. I was staring at the rolls of fat that made up its neck, and opening my mouth as it rounded, confused and pissed off at my unintentional trickery. As it turned and opened its mouth to roar again, I saw that inside, a sickly orange light like that of a Halloween pumpkin glowed at the back of its throat. The demon looked down and I leaped to my right just in time to avoid a gust of fire that came from its mouth, the strange, center fang hanging like an icicle and parting the fire so that it came out as twin blasts. I smelled the singe of fur and felt a gust of heat on my backside, but didn't give the monster time to compose itself before I was leaping and sinking my fangs into the loose, spongy flesh of its throat.

It tumbled backward, its head hitting a rock. Pieces of meat flew from the back of its skull like an over-ripened peach and I opened my mouth farther, sinking my fangs in until the flesh pushed at my gums. I hissed through my pointed teeth, almost letting go as smoky, acidic blood burned my sandpaper tongue, but it was over before the thing could even lift his arms to try to rip me off. The demon's body deflated like a balloon, flesh melting between my teeth and muscle falling from all of its bone. I tried to spit and backed away on my wide paws, shaking my head as the burn in my mouth spread to my throat. It hurt, bad, but I watched as the demon was reduced to a black odorous puddle that was quickly disappearing, smoking into nothing.

I sat down on my rump, stretching my limbs out before me, and lying down on the forest floor, wiping at my fur-covered face with the back of my paw white hot pain seared through my entire mouth. My tongue was on fire and I wondered if it would be reduced to goo like the demon's in front of me. My calf burned too, but not with the fiery ferocity of the blood that sank into my gums and seemed to be ripping them from the bone.

I tried to scream, but instead what came out was a throaty, mewling sound. I rolled in agony, wiping my face over and over again on the leafy floor of the valley, and struggled to remember what had ever driven me to attack the beast. I felt the tingle that signaled my shifting, but pushed it away. I didn't want to be naked and vulnerable in the woods, not now.

"You'll heal. You really didn't need to hang on that long. A simple bite would have done the job. After you do this a few times, you won't even feel the effects of their blood. It burns like hell at first, but you'll get used to it. I saw that leap, a couple of inches short and you would have a demon horn lodged in your stomach now. Sloppy, but you're new. It's to be expected."

I stopped thrashing, feeling the burn ease a bit, and looked up. Trace stood in above me in black nylon shorts that hit just below the knee. He was wearing an oversized white T-shirt that hung below his waist and he was staring at the puddle that had been a horrific deer-man just moments ago. His locket caught the moonlight and his vivid-green eyes burned into me like the monster's blood had done.

I felt my legs becoming human once again but Trace stooped down, grabbed my furry chin in his hands and leveled his gaze with mine. I saw his eyes flash with a brief challenge but he shook his head, just once, and kept his voice level.

"Don't shift back yet, it'll slow down the healing process a lot more. You think you're hurting now? Trust me. You don't wanna go there." He let go, standing back up, and I breathed heavily as I let the panther have full control once more.

I tried to whimper, but instead what came out was a high-pitched purring noise. Moments ago I'd been completely content in the furry hide of my inner animal, but now I just wanted my human body back so I could thrash and scream in a language Trace could understand, so I could ask him to make it stop, to knock me out, to kill me and put me out of my misery. I shook my large black head, watching smoke rise from my long, bloody whiskers.

I rolled onto my side, panting, my back paws pedaling into the earth. I don't know how long it went on, the burning that I knew had come straight from hell, but as the agony slacked down to something just outside of tolerable, I became aware that Trace was holding me.

"There, there. It's all right. It's all right, pretty." He sounded so old then, and I was morbidly amused when I recalled him saying he was pushing ninety years old. Strange, how while he held me, the thought didn't creep me out. After all, he didn't look much older than me, and as the pain lessened and I remembered what I'd been running from, I felt much older than he really was. I pulled from the warm, soothing comfort of his arms, realizing with a start that it was the safest I'd felt in a long, long time.

I had to tell him what I'd given permission to Laylian to do. I had to tell him about the unspeakable deed I'd set into motion. The panther was slipping away, stretching its angled limbs and yawning, satisfied, its bloodlust appeased.

No, no, no, no, no!

And for the second time that night, Trace saw me naked. I gasped, pulling my legs to my chest and crossing my ankles. His face had changed. Earlier I'd seen concern, maybe even a little kindness as he'd held my feline body in his arms, stroking my fur, but the instant I changed back, a sparkle had ignited in the chocolate depths of his eyes and his sensual lips had quirked at the corner. "My...aren't you a little morsel?"

I flipped him the bird, gesturing toward his shirt. At first he pretended to be confused by my request then, laughing softly, he took off the huge white tee and tossed it unceremoniously in my direction. His washboard stomach rippled, and the muscles in his shoulders flexed as he settled back onto the ground, legs stretched out, black sneakers twitching back and forth as if to a tune only he could hear.

I slipped the shirt over my head and stood, shoeless and feeling a very obvious breeze touching my bare ass. He probably got a good peek at everything I had as I pushed myself to my feet, but I didn't really care. In less than twenty-four hours I was already becoming used to being naked in front of strange men. If Mom had been alert, she would have been absolutely bursting with pride.

Mom.

I looked down at Trace and felt a blush creep into my face he stared appreciatively at my bare legs. I cleared my throat, lifting my chin and putting my hands on my hips.

"I'm gonna start charging peep show rates if you don't stop. We need to talk. I...it's about my mom...my mom, and Laylian."

He let his head loll to the side, something rippling just below the surface of his skin for a moment. I suddenly felt like Little Red Riding Hood, but without the granny or the desire to pick flowers. *Oh, Trace! What nice abs you have!* His posture relaxed and he lifted his brows as if to say, 'Go on'.

I started tapping one bare foot when his stare didn't

divert from my thighs and he snorted, rolling his eyes "It's nothing I haven't seen before. I've been watching you for a few weeks. Four, to be exact. Pearl had a vision and asked me to check you out. I've kept close tabs since, and the local shifter community is practically salivating for a chance to work with a tracker. Pearl likes to gossip. Oh… stop blushing. I've seen that you…get around. You've had your shirt off for more guys than I could shake a stick at."

He actually picked up a small dry twig and shook it, a mean gleam in his eye, his lips quirking up at the corners in a sneer.

My face burned. I felt the sudden, overpowering urge to defend myself. So what if I'd made out with random guys? Why was it any of his business?

"I'm not a whore, Trace, so kindly shut the hell up. You obviously haven't been spying on me thoroughly, or you'd know that it never went much further than that with any of them. Just shut up! How creepy are you? What? You've been peeping through my window? Hiding out on old mining sites while I steamed up some windows? What? Have you been beating it from the bushes? Just leave me alone!"

The valley was a banquet of musty, fertile scents. I could smell the decay of the leaves below my bare feet, and something I couldn't quite place, but that I knew was some type of woodland creature. My eyes zoomed in on his own, my vision so spectacular that I could have easily counted the hairs on his eyebrows in the moonlight. It was kind of dizzying, and I swayed a little on my feet, pulling at the bottom of the tee, making it as long as possible.

I took a deep, cleansing breath, telling myself that what he thought didn't matter, that the violation of my privacy was insignificant compared to what was going on back at the farmhouse, that as soon as I figured out this mess I would tell Trace to go off himself and tell Pearl that I wasn't joining the shifter community, that I would not kill demons or vampires or whatever kind of freaks they exterminated for the rest of my life. Mom would be alive, different, but alive. Laylian seemed to have self-control, and although creepy and rude, he didn't strike me as a merciless monstrosity. Maybe I was wrong, but I knew my mother, and she would never allow herself to become like the things in the old mine. She and I could run away, vanish, and leave Perry County to whatever fate it had in store. So what if she wouldn't exactly be human anymore? Neither was I. That didn't mean that we couldn't build a new life. That didn't mean that we had to stay here. I'd made a deal with Laylian, and I planned to follow through and lead him to the nest of rogue vampires, but after that I was taking my mother and leaving, whether she wanted to or not.

And as much as I despised Trace for his belittling remarks, I had to come clean. I could possibly need his help before all of this blew over.

"Laylian came to my house, to my mom's room, and he made a deal with me. He said that if I helped track down the rogue vampires he'd make my mom better. He said… he said he'd give her eternal life and swore that she'd be pampered. He's going to save her—then she and I are leaving."

His face contorted with anger and what looked like disgust, and he shifted smoothly over the span of a single beat of my heart, becoming the huge, white wolf with the thick, snowy fur and the long, wicked snout. It happened so quickly that I would have said it hadn't happened at all had I not been hit by the smell and almost knocked over by the force of the sudden blast of magic.

Then, just as quickly as he'd transformed into his wolf, he shifted back to his human form. His eyes, once again stared out of his beautiful, angry face. His next words made my empty tummy—unless you count demon blood—fall into my feet, and I knew I'd been wrong, very wrong.

"You little imbecile. When, tell me when? Is that why you ran out? Was he already drinking from her? Do you have any idea what kind of life you've damned her to?"

I was crying then, tears pouring from my eyes and gliding fat and warm down my cheeks. "Oh God. I don't know! I don't know anything about any of this crap. All I know is that my mom is dying and he told me he could save her and she'd live a happy life if I agreed to help. Don't judge me! You don't know what it's like. She's a good woman, she's not gonna be—"

He finished for me. "She's not gonna be a monster like the things you saw in your vision? Think again, Wren. She's going to need human blood to survive and drinking donated blood or not, do you think any sane person would consider that a life? She'll still be dead, but worse. You honestly believe in this childish fantasy of yours? You think you're gonna walk in, take her hand, and run away with her? And even if she was able to control her bloodlust long enough to indulge you, where would you go, huh? Wren! She won't even be able to tolerate sunlight. You can never have a life together. You are no longer capable of protecting her. I pity you, for you're in for a rude awakening. All you've done is create a new way to hurt yourself. You seem to have a knack for that."

I turned then, feeling my head tingle, feeling the rumbling in my chest. I wanted to shift again, so I'd have an excuse to avoid this all-too-human conversation, but my sadness held on tight, refusing to peel away enough for the big cat inside to take over.

Then Trace was taking me roughly by the arm and guiding me through the trees. Sharp little broken twigs poked at my feet and my legs itched terribly with that icky, crawly sensation you get when you've been, well, naked in the woods. He finally released me, leaving me to keep up on my own shaky limbs, but I wasn't too grateful. I stumbled trying to keep up with his long-legged stride. I tried not to watch the way his skin rippled over his bare back, or how the muscles in his calves bunched up with every step. It was the last thing I should have been doing, lusting over some strange ninety-year-old man who looked young enough to have graduated with me.

When we reached the top step of my front porch, he yanked me behind him, cocking his head and listening. He'd gone eerily, inhumanly still, more wolf than man. I could almost see his ears perk up. He held up one hand, a signal for me to be quiet, and that's when I heard it too. My new improved hearing had no trouble distinguishing who was the owner of that sweet, velvety voice.

A voice I hadn't heard in a very long time.

I felt like I'd been punched in the gut, and I made a wild lunge from behind Trace's bare back. I cursed as he grabbed me from behind, his forearm pushing hard against my soft belly, causing my breath to *whoosh* out. I dug my claws into his arm and he opened his mouth in a soundless grimace. He recovered quickly, pushing me back against his warm, firm chest and covering my mouth with his hand. I thought about biting down, but before I could he'd pressed his lips to my ear. His breath tickled as he whispered, "The woman you hear is not the same woman you knew. She's going to be different, Wren, and probably pretty unhappy that you've turned her into a bloodsucking monster. She's newly turned, and the newborns are the most dangerous of all. I don't think Laylian would allow her to attack you, but then again, I wouldn't have thought he would have been so foolish as to bribe you into letting him turn her in the first place. We don't know what we're going into, Wren. You could very well die if you barrel in there with your guard down I won't let your foolish love get you killed when she tries to rip your jugular out."

I cried quietly against his hand, sagging against his chest, wishing I could take it all back. What if she hated me? What if she went insane and sucked half the town dry? What if she didn't remember me? I feared I'd created a monster. I had a mental image of Mom with a chipped wineglass, laughing into the ear of the albino vampire as his followers rationed every last drop of blood from the victims stacked to the side on the earthen floor of the old coal mine. My nails, which I'd nibbled off just that morning, had somehow miraculously grown in length dramatically, because I was able to dig them into my palms to keep from screaming. I was horrified at the possibility that she could be a monster, but still, the little girl inside me held on to the hope that at any moment she'd open the front door and walk out, arms wide and looking just as flawless and fair as she'd been a few months ago.

Trace kept his hand pressed firmly against my mouth until, on impulse, I bit down. Moving quicker than I'd ever thought possible, I elbowed him in the gut and pushed away. I heard his air leave in an *oof* and I ran to the front door, threw it open and barreled straight into Oz's chest.

He staggered, his arms reaching up to catch my shoulders. His big, brown eyes were even wider than they'd been when I'd turned into the black panther for the first time in front of him, and his fingertips sank in hard. I looked down at his hand pointedly, my body trembling so much that my teeth chattered, and saw that his knuckles had gone white.

"Wren...I...I tried to wake your aunt, I didn't know what else to do when I couldn't find you. But it's like she's...it's like she's drugged. She's breathing, but she's not waking up. I was in your room then I heard...screaming. Lots of screaming. It's your mom. Th-the creepy guy from the cabin is in there, and he's done something. I don't know what the fuck he's done, but she was screaming. I tried to go in there to...I don't know, do something, but he pushed me out and locked the door. Your mom...she was...she was..."

His lips, usually deep, rosy red, had gone pale. His blond hair had fallen into his eyes, and his fingers bit in deeper into my shoulders. He was freaking out on me, and from the looks of the boy I wondered if he was going to faint. I could relate, and wondered which one of us would crumple to the floor first. I reached up, stronger than he even in my terrified state, and pried one of his hands free.

"She was what, Oz? Tell me." I tried to make my voice sound commanding, but it came out as a thick, mucus-

111

filled whisper. Trace chose that moment to walk in. He was breathing heavily and wrenched me backward by the back of the huge white T-shirt. I saw Oz's eyes shift down for a second, and though pale and shaken, a delicate blush gave his cheeks some much needed color. I'd probably pulled a Paris Hilton, but I didn't give a shit.

I whirled on Trace and pushed him backward. "Stay the fuck away from me! That's my mom in there, and she may need my help!" But he was dragging me toward the door, pushing it farther open with the toe of his sneaker, jaw set and determined.

"You're not going in there, Wren. You have no idea what you've done." He ducked his chin so he could level his gaze with my own. I struggled in his grasp, but I was growing weak. My sudden burst of adrenaline was dissipating at an alarming rate, and I felt a huge wave of guilt roll over me as I realized I was starving. Here I was, partially naked, with my aunt in some enchanted sleep in the back and my mother being converted into a creature of the night, and my belly was begging for sustenance.

Trace sighed, jerking me to his chest. He wrapped his fingers around my wrists and held them so that they were almost under my chin. I looked up into his strange green eyes, my breasts pressed against the iron of his body and tried to wrench free, but it was useless. The panther was no longer clawing at my soul. It had no desire to come out and play. Instead, it sat lazily in the corner, tail swishing, dozing. I felt all too human again, vulnerable, self-conscious. It was so different from the murderous hate-filled ferocity I'd felt as I'd torn into the neck of the cloven-hoofed demon. I felt flu-like, nauseous, and the room spun dizzily as my eyes settled on Trace's lips. They were pressed together firmly, and he breathed deeply in through his long, strong nose.

"Please," I croaked, the one word sounding more broken that I could ever remember sounding.

"I'm sorry," he whispered, looking behind me and scanning the room. "Let me try to explain this a little better.

112

Your mother is a newly made vampire. She's going to be confused and overwhelmed by the sudden changes in her senses, and most likely terrified to discover she's awakened from a dying, comatose body to find a strange, red-eyed man in her room. It's not like you see in the movies, the change doesn't take effect over a few hours, or even days. The transformation is complete in mere minutes. She's also going to be...hungry, and she may try to attack the first warm-blooded thing she sees. Do you want to be forced to defend yourself? Do you want to shift and be forced to either bite her or die? She'll be very strong, Wren. Vampires have amazing strength. Couple that with fear, and the combination is like dynamite. She needs to be removed immediately—I'm sure Laylian is in the process of doing so. Don't you hear her, Wren? Seeing you would only confuse her further. The only being she'll listen to now is her maker. Exchanging blood creates a bond. She'll listen to him, not you."

I began to shake my head but then my ears perked up. A high, keening sound was coming from the right side of the house—her bedroom. I could also hear Laylian speaking in soft, soothing tone, the type of low, calm voice one would use on a wounded animal or a toddler who's scraped their knee. I couldn't be sure, but I thought I heard Oz crying softly behind me. I was shaking so hard that I was bending at the waist, trying to fold into myself, but Trace's grip on my wrists prevented that.

Then I heard her speak, really speak. I still can't tell you what it was like, hearing her clearly for the first time in weeks.

"Wren," she repeated over and over, her pitch heightening each time she said my name. I could hear Laylian's voice, too, voice rising, reasoning, telling her to stay calm, that everything was going to be all right, that everything would be explained shortly. She sounded terrified, and I bit down hard on my tongue to keep from screaming. I tasted my own salty blood and I swallowed it down in a gulp, gasping

113

for air. Then a lot of things happened at once.

I'd never headbutted anyone intentionally, it had just always looked really painful in movies, but the need to see my mother—to see what was happening—took over my body. I headbutted Trace in the nose with my forehead, a sharp thud of pain vibrating in my skull and jarring my teeth. Upon impact I heard a distinct crack and knew that I'd messed his nose up pretty badly, but the apology would have to wait. He was the only thing standing between me seeing my mother awake again—an obstacle in the path to relief. I whirled, seeing Oz lunge for me but falling just short of my arm. My strength returned as if her voice were a shot of adrenaline directly into my heart, and my padded feet were soon slapping the tile of the kitchen, my long chestnut hair tangling over my eyes and whipping around my shoulders. I grabbed for the doorknob to her room and found that it was locked. I didn't pause before I was slamming my shoulder against it, once, twice, putting every ounce of strength I had into the blows. I would have some major bruising later, but I didn't care. All that mattered lay just behind the wooden barrier, and I had decided that I would see her or die trying.

I heard shouting, and with one last thump, the door swung wide. I glanced over my shoulder for just a second and saw Oz and Trace running toward me, bumping into each other in their haste.

Then I was inside, panting, half naked, and staring into the stormy gray eyes of the woman I had given up for dead. The hospital gown she wore was hanging off one shoulder and the bulge in her head was gone. Her hair, sweaty and sticking to one side of her angelic, pale face stuck out crazily on the other side. Her full lips were moving, reminding me of a fish out of water, and Laylian was holding her forearm firmly. Her knees were bent and a tangle of tubes and wires lay at her feet. Dried blood crusted one arm where she'd obviously ripped out her IV, but the bruises that had covered her flesh after many pricks with many different

114

needles were now gone, the skin pale and unblemished.

Her lips trembled and she raised one slender, small hand to her forehead. Her mouth slowly pulled back from her teeth, her eyes never leaving mine, and I saw the two, tiny fangs that told me all I needed to know. Her knees almost buckled and I wondered how she was standing after being bedridden for so long. Her bare legs had plumped out to their normal shapeliness, though they had been thin with disuse the last time I'd seen her. She wailed shrilly, and I knew I'd remember that sound until my dying day.

She shook her head. "Wren…Wren…what's happening? I…I could hear you. I could hear you telling me crazy stories, but I couldn't answer. I was…I was sick? Right? I have cancer. A tumor. Wren? Who is this man? Wren… Am I dead?" She was whispering now, with her eyes so wide they appeared to be bulging out of her skull. Once she brought her other hand up in front of her face. She lifted it close to her eyes, only to draw it away several times. She gasped, trembling so hard that her body pitched forward. Laylian tried to steady her with his hands around her waist and she grunted with effort as she struggled to take air into her lungs.

Then she went still, her breathing stopping, her back straightening as she pulled herself upright. She brushed Laylian's hands away idly. She sniffed the air and her head whipped in my direction. Her eyes were no longer a soft, stormy gray but red and fever-bright. I walked toward her, almost tripping over my numb feet.

"Mom?" The sound was full of hope. I didn't care that her eyes were blazing a hellish red. I didn't care that she was straining to break away from Laylian or that her lips were drawing back again from the wicked fangs where her human eyeteeth should have been. In that moment I was a six-year-old girl expecting a hug from my mommy, who would never, ever hurt me. Mommy, who could make everything all right.

Laylian was shouting something, pulling my mother

back, then strong arms were pulling me backward. I was pulled quickly from the bedroom and Oz dashed out to slam the door shut.

"You little fool! I told you. I told you what would happen!" Trace shouted against my ear.

I went limp in his arms and he pulled me away, my feet dragging against the tile. Then he scooped me up as if I weighed nothing and my arms instinctively went around his warm neck, his hair sliding like silk against the back of my hand as he moved quickly through the house. I heard Oz's footfalls behind us, but he didn't speak.

Chapter Ten

Ready or Not

Oz must have fetched me some shorts because suddenly Trace was helping me get them on, completing the task like he dressed semi-conscious girls every day. I was laid gently in the small backseat of Mom's Beetle, and I heard both boys settle into the front seats. Trace was holding one of my hoodies to his nose and he sniffed occasionally from the passenger side. I grimaced when he pulled it away bloody, remembering the headbutt I'd given his face earlier. He glared at me and pushed the fabric back to his nostrils.

"Drive," he told Oz, but Oz just sat there with his lip ring gleaming in the sparse light given off by the electronic dash. I tried to push myself up, failed, and fought to keep my eyes open.

"I said...drive." Trace spoke through gritted teeth, his voice muffled by the hoodie pressed to his face.

"But...but that was Wren's mom, man. We can't...we can't just leave her." Oz's voice trembled, but his hands never reached for the ignition.

Trace sighed, arm shooting out and turning the key for him. "That *was* Wren's mother, once upon a time, but not anymore. Right now, she's a newly awakened vampire and you guys are the all-you-can-eat buffet. It's not her fault—she's infected—but it doesn't change the fact that she's dangerous."

"But...but my aunt. She's still in there. She's still in there!" *Oh God, how could I have forgotten Aunt Mag?* She was lying somewhere in there in some vampire hypnosis-induced

117

sleep, helpless as a newborn kitten with its paws tied, and here we were, ready to flee as fast as the car would allow.

Trace twisted around in his seat, pulling the hoodie away from his nose. He pulled himself closer by the headrest, and pointed his finger. "You are *not* going back in there. If Laylian is wise, he's moving your mother already. We can't risk your life, you're leaving, and I'm going with you to make sure you don't do anything else foolish."

I managed to sit up, and leaned forward until my face was inches from his. I spat each word, mimicking his pointing finger and squinted my eyes, "I'm not leaving her with two vampires! Why should I take orders from you? I barely know you! Ever since you've come into my life it's been a crazy mess. I'm going back in, like it or not!"

His mouth twitched and his jaw bulged as he gritted his teeth. He opened the passenger-side door and tossed my hoodie into the back seat. It landed on my arm and I pushed it away when I realized it was soaked with his blood.

His voice sounded tired and exasperated. "Laylian won't allow her to be harmed — you're useful to him. He wants to please you. Your mother is now his responsibility. I don't trust him very much, but he's never gone back on his word as far as our business is concerned." Trace slid out of the door, stretched his back with his hands on his hips, then cupped his chin with his hand and jerked his head sharply to the right, cracking his neck audibly. I shuddered.

He opened my door and motioned for me to get out. "Your aunt is sleeping like a baby. Your mother and Laylian are gone. Come back inside, clean up, get some rest."

"How can you be sure?" I asked

"I can smell them when they're near. You should be able to as well." He said it as if this was common knowledge. I sniffed, noticing that the peculiar death and flowers scent I was becoming used to was no longer strong. It faded even as I inhaled, and I shook my head. I got out slowly, my legs feeling stiff and rubbery, and avoided Trace's eyes. Oz wasn't with us, not really. The lights were on but no one was home. He stared out of the windshield, jaw slack. I walked around to the driver's side, opened the door and gripped his shoulder. His eyes widened and he snapped back into alertness as if waking from a dream.

After we were inside I checked on Aunt Mag in her room upstairs, feeling something tightly wound in me loosen a little as I watched her breath deeply and evenly. She was curled up in a thick faux fur throw, and she sighed as the light from the hall spilled across her face. But as soon as I shut her door a horrible realization dawned on me. Whenever Aunt Mag woke up, my mother would be gone. Not gone as in dead, but mysteriously absent. We both knew Mom wasn't anywhere near well enough to get up and walk out. Hell, she hadn't even been well enough to keep her eyes open, so my poor aunt would assume that someone had kidnapped her or that her pothead charge had had something to do with it.

Oh. Shit.

I showered in the upstairs bathroom as quickly as possible, not bothering to use conditioner in my hair even though I knew that meant a wickedly bad hair day tomorrow. I burst into my room, loose jersey shorts and black and white checked tee feeling cozy and warm. Now that I wasn't covered in blood and dirt, I was ready to talk. Amazing how something as simple as a hot shower can change your total outlook on things.

Trace was standing in the far left hand corner, inspected one of the little glass pigs I secretly collected. I had at least fifty glass pigs hidden under my bed, but I wouldn't tell him that.

Oz stood at the window, his fair hair shimmering in the soft light my lamp cast. His hands were in the back pockets of his jeans and he bent his neck from side to side, trying to work out a kink of some sort.

I didn't waste time, I got right to the point. "Okay — so I have roughly a million questions for you, Trace, but right now, this particular one takes the cake." I walked over and

119

plopped down on the end of my bed, knees bouncing with nervous energy. I pushed a wet, wavy lock of hair behind my ear.

Trace put the pig back on the small nightstand and turned to face me, crossing his muscular arms over his bare chest. Good lord, the boy was built. I could see the wolf just beneath the surface in the way his eyes darkened when he focused his attention fully on me. He was a live wire, a bungee cord ready to break. His skin seemed to ripple with barely contained violence and I shivered, wondering if I found him more threatening in his wolf or human form. His long white shorts had slid a little farther down, revealing muscles creating a vee at his hips. Tendons stood out on his shoulders and even though none of this was really his fault if I looked at it from afar, his smug expression made me want to punch him in his once broken nose, which now wasn't even swollen.

"I broke your nose," I told him, not sounding convincing even to myself. I'd heard the snap of bone when I'd headbutted him. I'd watched him bleed.

He shrugged, his green eyes darkening just a little. "I heal fast. Thank you for that, by the way. I try to protect you and what do you do? You headbutt me in the face. Given the circumstances, I'll let that one go, but if you—"

"Stop right there," Oz snarled, turning from the window and shooting Trace a look that actually made me hold my breath. I opened my mouth to say something, anything, to change the subject, because I had the feeling that things were about to go from bad to worse. Oz wasn't a fighter, and Trace was, well, Trace—a nearly century-old shapeshifter who could change from seemingly human boy into a giant white wolf in seconds.

Trace turned his head slowly, too slowly. "You have no authority here, kid. The only reason I'm allowing you to stick around is because your presence seems to have a soothing effect on Hellion here. The wise thing for you to do is sit down and let those who are higher on the food

120

chain talk business."

I sprang to my feet quicker than I could have a few nights ago, but I wasn't quick enough. Oz, the boy who had been the one to cry while watching *Titanic* and who had rescued butterflies from spider webs in sixth grade, Oz, who had been bullied relentlessly by every football or basketball player in the county and had let it roll of his shoulders, did something I'd have thought he wasn't capable of. He actually threw the first punch.

My vision zoomed in on his eyes, the tear ducts tilting upwards just slightly, his soft, full lips becoming a hard, red slash. Then he smiled, a joyless thing that filled me with guilt. Before all of this, Oz would have never have smiled that way. When he smiled it was genuine, and I realized with a tiny flutter in my stomach, any real smile from him was usually reserved for me and me alone.

Everything slowed down, and I saw him take two slow steps toward Trace. The glass pig watched this all with an expression of cute surprise from its perch on the small shelf and I had the crazy urge to run and move it before it was broken in whatever scuffle was about to unfold. Mom had shoved the glass piggy into my stocking just last Christmas with a tiny note that had said *Probably not the kind of bacon you were expecting. But I'm still cute, right?*

But Oz's bunched, bony fist never met its mark. Trace stepped back easily and Oz's fist shot gracelessly through the air, missing my pig by inches. I shrieked and jogged toward them with my palms out in a calming gesture, as if by will alone I could make them hug and say they were sorry. My body tingled and I realized I was pissed – really pissed. My mom had just tried to eat me and the two of them chose this moment to have a testosterone war?

Trace shifted and the tingle that signaled my change fizzled out abruptly. The shorts he was wearing slid into a pool on the carpet and I'd have bet my life that if they had been jeans, he would have ripped right out of them. The thought wouldn't have been so bad under different circumstances, but right now I had no interest in his physical qualities. He growled deep in his chest and used one large paw to push the shorts out of the way. Wolves are huge, I knew that, I'd seen them on television, but the furry white beast before me made them all look like purse puppies. His beast was unlike anything in the wild, from the tufts of hair pointing skyward on his huge, perked ears to the saucer-sized paws that slammed into Oz's back, pushing him down. The bones in his wide snowy shoulders jutted out as he bent his shaggy satellite dish head down beside of Oz's cheek. His upper lip lifted, revealing large, thick teeth that were wickedly sharp on the ends — made for ripping flesh from bone. He snorted from his wet black nose and the human green eyes blazed. Saliva dripped from his lower jaws and he barked like a wild dog over its fresh kill, signaling that it'll rip the throat out of any other creature that tries to stake a claim on its meal.

Oz went motionless, palms flat, breathing heavily. His bucked just once, realized that the two hundred-pound thing on his back wasn't budging, then pressed his cheek against the floor. I could see he tried to keep his expression outraged instead of scared, but he was failing. That look was all I needed.

I picked up the only thing I could find, an old lava lamp on my dresser that I hadn't hooked up in years. I willed my beast to take over, but it didn't. I was too shaken, too torn, and dominance rolled from the big white wolf in electric waves. Oz made a pained sound and he gasped, his eyes growing wide when he looked up at what I was holding in my shaking hands.

Trace must not have noticed, because he kept growling against Oz's cheek. I knew what he was doing, he was trying to terrify him into submission, to make him go along with whatever he said, just like he was trying to bully me.

I smacked him upside the head, the lava lamp shattering with the strength of my blow. Water and neon-colored goo soaked his snow-white fur, and I had the satisfaction of seeing his eyes widen for a moment in cartoonish surprise.

"Get off of him, mutt—unless you want a death match. He's not the intruder here, you are. Every time something goes wrong lately, you're conveniently right in the middle of it." I dropped the base of the ruined lamp, waiting for him to budge, but he responded with a snarl, with skin pulling back from his brindled gums and saliva dripping from the tips of his incisors.

"Stop, Wren. I'm okay! I'm okay," Oz assured me while he gasped in-between words. I lifted my fist, then I felt the tingle. I felt pinpricks in my palm and opened it in front of me, seeing the bright red crescents where my glossy new nails had broken the skin. The need to be in control was too much and my panther gave a high-pitched, murderous scream of rage, an instinct to protect what was mine. The realization that I thought of Oz as my own stilled the change for a moment. A million questions popped into my head— was that what was happening? Was I beginning to think of Oz as more than my best friend? Did it really even matter in the middle of all of this chaos? I planted my feet firmly and threw back my head, waiting for the panther to take over. Waiting to punish Trace for daring to harm what was mine.

The door opened. Aunt Mag stood in a T-shirt and flannel bottoms, looking suspiciously refreshed with her hair braided neatly and falling over her impressive shoulder. She actually smiled, the first genuinely positive expression I'd seen in weeks, and looked as if she were ready to say something just as chipper. That was, until she saw that freakishly large white wolf growling over Oz, who was looking at her with more terror than he'd shown when he'd been flattened to the floor by a crazy shapeshifter. I stared at him, waiting for him to come out with a clever explanation.

Something like—"Oh, hey, Mag! I've been short on cash so I've been dog sitting. What? Is he hurting me? Nah. This is how we play. What is he? Oh…he's a polar mix. A really big breed. Doesn't he sorta remind you of a polar bear? Never mind the broken glass, he gets a little excited."

But instead he squeaked, sounding as if he'd just wet his pants. Trace wasn't snarling, but his mouth actually hung open, his green human eyes screaming *wrong* in the canine face. He couldn't have looked more unnatural if he'd tried.

I looked at Aunt Mag, her jaw on the floor, and she slowly turned her head, her eyes meeting mine.

"Wren…would you like some ice cream?"

Then she fell into a dead faint.

Trace had shifted back, and I caught a glimpse of a smooth, muscular butt before he was shimmying his way into his shorts. I was shrieking at him hysterically and Oz was pacing uselessly, running his large, bony hands through his soft, golden hair over and over again.

"This was gonna be the topic of discussion before you two hormonal idiots decided to trade licks! What do I tell her about Mom? How do I explain *you*? She's not gonna believe that you were just a normal dog. She's not a total imbecile! Oh, my God. She's gonna die. How do I explain this? What in the sugar-coated hell am I going to do?" I was fanning her face with a teen fashion magazine with her head in my lap. Her eyes fluttered over and over and she was muttering unintelligibly. I facepalmed.

"Just kill me — please," I told no one, wishing I could curl so tightly into a ball that I could disappear and not have to deal with the monumental task before me. Poor Aunt Mag. She'd left her shop, dropped everything, and come here to assist her sister in being as comfortable as possible with a terminal illness. Couple that with being left with a wayward, bitter eighteen year old, and you can assure yourself of a constant headache. And now? Now she would wake up and I'd have to try to explain that my unresponsive mother was missing and make up something feasible about the huge wolf she's seen. I didn't want to lie. I was perfectly fine with lying about my whereabouts when I came dragging in too late at night, or telling her that the pot she smelled was just from the smoking stoner I'd walked by on the street, but my stomach jittered violently when I thought about lying

124

to her about any of this.

It felt so wrong. She deserved better.

"You can't involve her," Trace said calmly, lacing his sneakers back up and rolling his head on his shoulders. Occasionally he'd glare at Oz, but I'd already informed them both that if they so much as sneezed in the each other's direction, I would beat them both with my one remaining lamp.

"It's a little too late for that, dontcha think?" Oz sneered as he walked over and knelt by Aunt Mag.

"Thanks to your suicidal tendencies, yes, it's made things a little more difficult than necessary," Trace said with a fake, tight grin.

I groaned, wishing I could shift and castrate him with my claws.

"Aunt Mag?" I said for the fifteenth time. She moaned but her eyes just kept fluttering. "What's wrong with her? I need to call a doctor!"

Trace snorted. "That's logical. Why don't you just backhand the hornet's nest? Spit on it, while you're at it? She's fine. She couldn't handle the perfection. Happens all the time."

I was going to rip his throat out.

Then her eyes flew open. She blinked a few times, her eyes growing wider and wider with each bat of her dark lashes. She looked from me to Oz and slowly turned her head toward my bed. Trace grinned and winked, as if he were greeting an old friend.

"Who is that, Wren? And why is he on your bed?" she whispered, as if Trace couldn't hear her.

Then she gasped. "The big dog! Where is that big dog? Oz, are you all right? I...I took a nap. I was just going to ask... Oz, answer me?"

Oz dropped his head and let his hands flop into his lap. I gazed heavenward. "I'd ask you to sit down, Aunt Mag, but I think you'd better just lay there for this one."

"Don't," Trace said, the one word so commanding that I

125

almost buckled and obeyed. I lifted my chin, taking Aunt Mag's hand.

"You're going to have to kill me if you don't want me to talk, Trace. It's the least I can do for her after...all of this."

Chapter Eleven

Denial

A whopper of an argument had followed, and I'd fought to keep my panther from clawing her way out. After I'd won, with Trace so annoyed that a vein had visibly throbbed at his temple, I had guided Aunt Mag downstairs and into the kitchen.

After she'd drunk four cups of coffee, hysterically screamed and nearly fainted again when she'd realized Mom was really gone, and pulled a butcher knife from the drawer when Trace and I had both shifted to prove our claims, Aunt Mag sat quivering in her kitchen chair, squeezing an empty coffee mug in her hands so hard that her knuckles turned white.

Oz cleared his throat, Trace paced like a caged animal and I sat there useless as I tried to give Aunt Mag time to process everything she'd just witnessed. One big, wet tear slid from her eye, making its way to the tip of her nose. My vision — enhanced randomly — focused on that tear as it quivered then splattered on the cherry tabletop.

"I...I don't believe — in vampires," she whispered for the twentieth time. "And I don't believe in magic. It's...the stress. I must be sick. I need you to drive me to the hospital, Wren. I'm... I don't know what's real anymore."

I sighed, resisting the urge to bang my forehead against the tabletop until I went unconscious.

"Damn it," I whined, and Aunt Mag came out of her fog just long enough to make a disapproving sound at my cursing.

"I know this sounds crazy...I thought it was just one big hallucination just a couple of days ago, but it's real, Aunt Mag. Mom walked out, healed, but...different. I'm a shifter. It's genetic, from my father. Shifters hunt...bad things. Things normal people never see. They're kind of everywhere."

Aunt Mag sniffled, wiping at her nose. "My sissy. I have to see her. If what you're saying is true, I have to see her with my very own eyes."

I started to explain that right now that would be a bad time, that Mom was gripped by bloodlust, but thought better of that. The last thing I wanted to do was scare Aunt Mag more. She knew what a vampire was supposed to be like, what they drank. She loved horror movies and had every Wes Craven film on DVD. It wasn't something that needed to be voiced.

"Trust me when I say that right now, that wouldn't be a good idea. Mom is...adjusting. She's not some evil creature of the night like you see in the movies, but she's having to learn how to live with her, um, new predicament. So please...just give me a little time, and I'll see what I can do."

The fog cleared from her eyes and they widened until they reminded me of red-tinted saucers. "You're not going to go searching for anything. I hope you know that. You're not leaving this house until we can sort out what's really happening here. The police need to be called."

"No!" Oz and I both shouted in sync. Trace just turned his back, letting his head drop to his chin. I heard him release a long, steadying breath.

I was trying to sound understanding, really, I was, but my voice sounded as annoyed as I felt. My patience was reaching its breaking point. "You can't do that, Aunt Mag. They'd never find her anyway. All that will accomplish is making everyone think you've gone nuts. Who's going to believe that a woman on her deathbed was transformed into a vampire? Really. Aunt Mag, think. I know it's a lot to take in, but I really, really need you to trust me right now."

She laughed humorlessly as she pushed her coffee mug to the side. "Trust you, Wren? The girl who didn't care what happened to her mother a mere two days ago? The girl who lies, and comes home smelling like weed? The girl who pulls into the driveway with a different boy every night of the week?" She was crying again, and she smacked the tabletop with her hand—hard. She leaned back, her brown curls coming loose from her braid and clinging to her temples.

I felt like I'd been slapped. Even the demon blood that had burned my tongue from the battle in the valley hadn't unsettled me this badly. I pushed away from the table, the legs protesting with a toothache screech, and turned my back on Aunt Mag. I took deep, even breaths, feeling the warning tingle.

I don't know who I said it to, but my voice cracked with every word. "Turns out, I'm a super special kind of shifter. I can shift into animals...but tonight I shifted into this clone of Laylian, fangs and all. He says that makes me valuable, and the way he looked at me..."

I hadn't even heard Trace move, but suddenly he was in front of me, grasping my shoulders tightly, pulling me so close that his breath tickled my nose. "Repeat that, Wren, because I know I couldn't have heard you right the first time."

Aunt Mag was still crying, still lost in her grief and fear and the conviction that she'd lost her mind. She hiccupped now and then, and I turned around to see if she was listening. The look on her face was so far away that I wasn't even sure she realized she was in the kitchen anymore.

I wrenched my shoulders free. "You heard me. I didn't stutter."

Oz noisily made his way to my side, and from the corner of my vision I could see him searching my face. "Whoa, you mean, you can shift into a vampire? What about other things, Wren?"

I looked over my shoulder at Aunt Mag, who had gone

129

back to holding her coffee cup and muttering in a high-pitched, breathy voice. I grabbed Oz's hand, leading him out of the kitchen and down the hall into the living room. Trace followed, still shirtless and looking furious at everyone and everything.

I put my hands on Oz's shoulders, pushing him back a couple of steps, adjusting him so that he was facing me perfectly. I reached up and touched his cheek, and for a second I marveled that there was actually stubble there. My vision zoomed in and I could see that his facial hair was as fair as the hair on his head, but had been recently shaved. I breathed him in, cheap department store deodorant spray and a scent that reminded me of excitement. I left my hand there for a moment, and oddly enough, discovered I liked it there. Then a wave of invisible attraction hit me. It rolled from Oz in one heaping dose. I saw a blush creep from his long, thin neck and slowly spread under my hand.

"Watch me," I whispered, and felt myself grow taller, narrower. The shorts I'd been wearing were now hilariously short and my tee several sizes too small. I smoothed my hand down my chest and felt my ribs poking through just below the surface through my shirt. I pushed silky blond hair out of my eyes, and took my hand away.

I looked at Trace, and wished I had a camera handy. His big green eyes were now wide and dumbfounded. With his mouth agape like that, he reminded me of a kid watching his first rated-R movie—enthralled, and happily melting his brain on the visuals.

Oz took a step back and I shushed him, thinking he would scream, but instead he just gave me a bright, sunny grin.

"Fail, Wren. You're missing the metal."

I reached up and found that, indeed, I had no piercings.

"Wow. This is weird. Ya know, I've kind of always wondered how others saw me, and now I know. Damn, I'm one ugly mother—"

"May God have mercy on your soul," Trace muttered, his face shifting into a look that could almost be mistaken for pity. "You have a hard row to hoe, shifter. Your net worth just burst through the roof as far as nasties are concerned."

I focused on a mental image of own face then, and seamlessly shifted back into my own skin. It was a weird sensation, shrinking. Everything had looked so different from a few inches higher.

Trace let out a low whistle, shaking his head and opening the front door.

"Wait!" I snapped, almost cutting myself short when I remembered I'd been wishing him gone just moments before. "Where are you going?"

Trace shrugged. "Pearl needs to hear this. This changes a lot of things. If word gets out—and it will—even with Laylian's good intentions, other…beings are going to take a huge interest in you. You're not going to be safe. We need to prepare accordingly."

I walked after him, putting my hand on the door and trying to close it back. "This is safe? How much worse can it get? Really?"

He stared blankly at the doorknob, then pried my hand away from the door effortlessly, stepping out into the night. "A shifter with the ability to transform into anyone's enemy, and a tracker to boot? Lots."

"So what are you gonna do about it?" My hands went instinctively to my hips in true pissed-chick fashion.

"I am going to discuss this with Pearl, and you're coming with me. Also, you'd probably do well to respect your deal with Laylian. He's all right for a leech, but he's very, very powerful. A married couple went missing tonight. Their teen son was lucky and escaped, he described them as being men with red, glowing eyes. His saving grace was the family dog, a Doberman to be exact. I'm surprised the news isn't being belted from the rooftops with a loudspeaker. The mayor is demanding that everyone stay indoors until the suspects are caught."

I felt my face crumble. I knew what would happen to the married couple, I'd seen what the rogue vampires did with their victims. I also knew that a portion of that blood would be on my hands, considering I had some weird, new inner GPS that would lead me right to their hideout so the powers that be could destroy them. Of course, it was very likely that the married couple was dead already. The tunnel dwellers hadn't seemed like a patient lot.

Then I felt Oz's hand on the small of my back, gently patting, soothing.

It wasn't just about me anymore. I had been given several...abilities. Why? I didn't quite believe in destiny. I had no damn clue. I was special, and that meant that there would always be someone coming for me, someone wanting to either kill me or hire me...or possibly both. Why not help? It wasn't as if I had anything to lose. My mom was not only dead, but undead, and Aunt Mag had momentarily gone off the deep end.

"We have to find Laylian. Tell him that if he wants to prevent two more slaughters he needs to get up with me — quick. I just want this over with, okay?"

Trace looked both unsettled and pleased at the same time. "I'm normally an assassin for cash, but this one I'd take on for free. I'm glad you're going to assist. You won't be involved in the nastier parts, I promise."

And somehow I believed him.

But before he could usher me out my arm shot out, firmly grasping his wrist but carefully avoiding digging in my brand spankin' new long, gleaming nails that would have made any hand model envious. "Aunt Mag."

Trace went still, giving me his full attention, and this time he was considerate enough to keep most of the mocking gleam out of his eyes. He tilted his head, waiting for me to go on. I could tell he was fighting the urge to tap his foot impatiently by the way he was twisting the heel of one sneaker into the carpet.

I didn't look away. "She can't stay here, Trace. We have to hide her until the worst is over. I can't leave her, that's basically hanging a big *Kidnap me!* sign around her neck.

Someone...or something...might try to use her to get to me."

"We have greater concerns right now. Listen to her, she's delirious, she won't go anywhere willingly. She's convinced she's mentally ill. You're right, it's not safe for her here, but it's even less safe for you. You could save a lot of lives, Wren, and we don't have time to play nursemaid." He spoke each word carefully, as if talking to a small child, and I tightened my grip, letting my nails scrape the delicate skin of his inner wrist. I felt a vein there, his blood traveling under my fingertips, and I wondered how someone so heartless could possibly have a heartbeat.

"The hell we're leaving her. You either help me get her to a safe place or the deal is off. Laylian can come back and mummify me for all I care, but I'm not abandoning her here. She deserves more than that after what I've put her through. What if it were Pearl, Trace? What if?"

I felt Oz standing closer now, the heat of his body and his own, unique smell like a balm to my nerves. I realized I could hear the slightly erratic beat of his heart and I tried to focus on something else. *Thump...thumpthump....thump.* My weird, new senses were proving to be super distracting.

Trace looked down at his wrist pointedly and I let go. With one jerky nod he left me, heading back into the kitchen.

It took me exactly two crying fits and a detailed description of what the rogue vampires could do before Aunt Mag would lift a single butt cheek from the kitchen chair. She was threatening to call the police again. I couldn't keep myself from thinking that it would be really convenient if I could tie her up and gag her without guilt. Soon we were bouncing and skidding up the hillside that led to Pearl's cabin, Aunt Mag sobbing the whole time and trying to convince me to let her out so she could run as far away from us all as possible. I tried to calm her, but she regarded me as if I had three heads and the mark of the beast on my forehead. I fully understood her reaction, but it didn't make things any less annoying.

133

Laylian was waiting on the small porch, but considerately faded into the shadows when he saw Aunt Mag trying to make a break for it.

When we made it inside Pearl took one look at Aunt Mag and bustled off to the kitchen. She returned with a mug full of 'special cider' and offered Aunt Mag a sweet, grandmotherly smile as she pressed the cup into her trembling hands.

"Bless your heart," she cooed to my aunt, voice dripping with honey and featherbed comfort. "It's gonna be all right, now. It's a lot to take in, I know." She rested her wrinkled hand on Aunt Mag's forearm, the effect like that of flicking a switch.

Aunt Mag smiled back, years vanishing from her drawn, worried face. She swayed a little, murmuring a mightily slurred thanks, and followed Pearl to the kitchen like an obedient grandchild. I shivered, wondering how the heck she did that, and decided not to dwell lest I lose my nerve for what was coming next. Before we'd left I'd changed into some jeans and a snug plain black T-shirt.

Oz had changed too, after I'd found one of his T-shirts I'd borrowed once when I'd gotten covered in Pepsi at his house. His shirt was blood red with a decal Oscar the Grouch from *Sesame Street* on the front. His wide, grumpy eyes peeked out from the top of a yellow garbage can, the lid tilting precariously on his head.

Trace remained shirtless, which was proving to be quite the distraction. With every graceful move the muscles of his back or chest would tighten and ripple under the surface. His olive skin had a natural glow, which gave him an almost airbrushed effect. Laylian chose that moment to materialize out of nowhere, causing both Oz and I to jump out of our skins. Trace didn't even flinch, obviously used to seeing vampires appear out of thin air.

I had barely recovered from the shock when my mouth decided to carry on without me.

"How's Mom? Where did you take her?"

134

Laylian smiled, going for the gentle, patient look, which was kind of impossible with his blazing, inhuman eyes.

"She's doing well. She's much calmer now that she's fed," Laylian informed me calmly.

I felt my knees get weak and my stomach gave an acidic lurch, "I think I'm going to be sick. Was that really necessary? And you didn't answer me, where did you take her?"

Laylian shook his head, just once, but sharply, "That's not important at the moment. After we've settled certain business matters, I'll bring her to you so you can see for yourself that she's safe and well. She's not staying against her will, if that's what you're wondering. She's been very open, and her transition has been seamless. She worries for you, and she's somewhat distressed about the…choice you made, but she seems to blame me for that entirely. She's linked to me in body and mind, and she hates me for it passionately. I do think that I'm already half mad with lust for her."

"That's interesting," I heard Oz mumble, and I shot him a look that should have been accompanied with a spray of venom.

"That's just super," I spat. "But my mom would never give you the time of day, she's…"

"Different? Human?" Laylian chirped. He looked mighty pleased with himself and was grinning like a fiend. I thought I recognized that look, and was surprised an undead freak such as himself could experience such emotions. The look was giddiness.

Ugh.

"Are we going to get on with this, or what?" I asked, wanting to steer as far away from the current subject as possible. I inhaled, smelling the unmistakable greasy, succulent scent of frying chicken. My stomach growled and I blushed.

"Pearl is making supper," Trace informed me. "It should be ready shortly."

135

My mouth filled with saliva. I couldn't remember the last time I'd eaten. "She's making supper, at midnight?"

Trace nodded as if it were the most common thing in the world.

Laylian cleared his throat. "While your aunt is manageable, let us go sit in the living area. I'm going to need you to use your talent, Wren. We need to determine the best time for the...cleansing. It would be terribly inconvenient if we showed up when they were gone. They'll be able to smell us, and would change camp and further complicate matters.

"It's in an old, deep abandoned mine. The coal companies usually take all the timbers out and let them collapse after they're done mining, but there's still some that are open. And this one looked really, really old. I-I can still sense them if I think about it. It's kind of like a string is pulling at my stomach...it's horrible. He's there, right now."

Somehow I was aware of him, his black aura passing over my consciousness. I felt his madness, his malice, and I pushed back, letting the weird, invisible fishing line attached to my stomach disconnect.

"I...I don't wanna go back there like I did earlier. I don't wanna see those people if the same thing happened to them that happened to the others, but I can tell you where he is. I'll take you there. But know this, after this, I'm done. You said I didn't have to be actively involved in killing those creeps, and I want someone protecting me while you do whatever it is you're planning. Okay?"

Laylian nodded, looking thoughtful. Something flashed through his red eyes that I couldn't put my finger on. It had flickered so quickly, in fact, that I really couldn't be certain I'd seen it at all. But I knew, yeah, I knew that this wasn't the end. Laylian was far too fascinated with me, too charmed by my weird abilities. Plus, he pretty much owned the one person in the world I was doing this all for. Looking at him, I supposed that it could be worse. Having someone powerful on my side at this point was probably a blessing in some ways.

"Go rest, eat, and be ready to lead myself and a few of my clan in an hour. Trace, I take it you're going to be in attendance as well?"

Trace snorted, and his voice was full of steel and barely contained hostility when he spoke. "I'm not leaving her side. I also request that we have several guards for Wren. She gets harmed in any way, Laylian, and I'm done with doing you favors. In fact, you won't be in a position to ask for my help if something happens to her. You'll be dust in the wind, my friend."

I looked at Trace with a mixture of shock and confusion. Did he really mean that? Did he care only because he thought I would be useful to the shifter community, or had he somehow grown slightly fond of me during our short time together? He'd saved my life, right? He'd insinuated that he'd been watching me for some time earlier, and the thought made me both blush and feel more than a little violated. Anger flared and I felt tingly all over. I pushed the panther back, knowing this wasn't the best time to get furry.

"Big promises for a stalker," I said, pointlessly. The words seemed to have the effect I'd been aiming for though, because he actually growled.

"What about me?" Oz asked, and I suddenly remembered he was there. He could have gone home and I wouldn't have held it against him, but he'd stayed, accepting all of the chaos and sticking by my side. He hadn't complained yet, and I was suddenly filled with warm gratitude that made my eyes threaten to water. Was he actually offering to go with us to the vampire den?

Laylian and Trace both opened their mouths to object but I beat them to it, knowing that it would go much smoother if I were the one telling him to stay behind. I turned, seeing a new stubbornness in his stance that hadn't been there yesterday, and I felt something alien and strange flutter in my stomach.

"No, Oz. I know I'm no more cut out for this than you are,

137

but I made a promise and, well, I can protect myself better than you if I have to. I don't want both of our lives at risk. Please…just stay with Aunt Mag. She needs a familiar face right now. I have to do this. If I don't, more people will die."

He shook his head, stepping closer and taking both of my hands in his. I could hear his heartbeat again and I felt a fierce protectiveness. Seeing him here, among one brute shapeshifter and one undead vampire, he seemed so fragile, so…human. I jerked a little, wondering when I'd began thinking of him like that, wondering at what point I had accepted I was something more complex.

"Fuck that, Wren. I'm coming. I'm not leaving you alone with that" — he jerked his head toward Laylian — "or that." He freed his hand and gestured toward Trace, who regarded him like he was a mosquito buzzing about the room, annoying, tiny and deserving of being splattered under his hand. He dropped his head. "You don't have to do this, you know?"

Laylian sighed, sounding bored, then spoke to Oz as if reading from a newspaper.

"Your assistance is not necessary. I can smell your blood from a mile away. We might as well stuff an apple in your mouth and prepare a spit to hang you on. You're vulnerable. If things go badly, Wren can shift and defend herself. You, however, would be a midnight snack. She needs to focus on getting us in, not on watching over you. She's still inexperienced, so this is risky enough without her bringing a pet along."

The snotty tone rubbed my nerves raw and I felt Oz's hand tighten with outrage. His emotions hit me hard — despair, fear and a feeling of uselessness. He'd been put in his place, and it hurt him. But what Laylian had said was true. Things could get bad really quick. How bad? I didn't know, and really didn't want to dwell because it would make me lose my nerve.

"You don't have to be such an ass about it." I spoke through gritted teeth. My jaw hurt I was clenching it so

138

hard. I'd had just about enough of cocky males. "Oz, he's right, to an extent. After tonight all of this will be over and we won't have to worry about crazy stuff like this. I'll get Mom and…"

Trace groaned, and I longed to punch him in his full, sensual mouth.

"But," Oz began, knowing that he'd lost. He sighed, searching my face for any indication that I still wanted to take him along. Begging me not to push him away with a sudden suspicious shimmering in his pretty brown eyes.

"You might get yourself killed—and me too. Please, just stay here. I'll be back soon, I promise." I stomped a little, reaching the whining stage.

After more detailed descriptions of the terrors that he would endure at the hands of barbaric vampires from Laylian and some threats from Trace that almost resulted in another pitiful attempt at an ass kicking from Oz, he finally gave up, but not before he stomped up to Trace and Laylian, pointing at each of them.

"You two let anything happen to her and I'll find a way to kill you. I swear. She'd better come back unharmed or I'll consider her blood on your hands. I'll burn this damn cabin down and make sure the witch is in it when I do."

Trace drew back his fist, but I jumped in-between them, feeling like ripping out my hair and stuffing both of their mouths with it.

"Shut up! Both of you. Now is not the time to be doing this again. Just get away from each other and go beat on your stupid monkey chests somewhere else! This has nothing to do with either of you. Laylian and I made a deal. This is *my* choice, and whatever happens from this point on is because I willingly followed through. Oz, go check on Aunt Mag. I want to go while the pull is still strong."

Oz obeyed, breathing hard and looking as if he could chew up iron and spit out nails. As he passed, he paused long enough to bend close and brush my cheek with his lips. It was featherlight, warm, and I shivered at the pleasant

139

sensation.

As he walked away I looked up and noticed Trace was staring at me, his eyes burning holes in my face. A hot blush crept into my cheeks and I rolled my eyes when he smirked. "Got a problem?" I asked, letting my arms fall loose to my sides.

"No. Not a problem," he said, voice sickly sweet, imitation velvet. "It's just so...cute. Have you touched his no-no stick yet? Babies. I see lots of babies in your future, some of them furry. With his blood, I wonder what their main animal would be? Probably the world's first bunny shifters. That's one sure way to kill the species off."

"Suck it," I said, flipping him the bird.

"You have one of those? You really are one of a kind. Fascinating."

"Laylian?" I growled. "Let's get this show on the road. I'd rather not kill another disgusting abomination tonight. Sidelines, remember?"

Laylian looked like he was watching the world's most entertaining sitcom. He was actually stroking his chin, smiling with just a peek of fang. He met my eyes, the dreamy look fading. He nodded, turned on his heel, and both Trace and I followed suit, being careful not to walk too closely to each other. In my current mood, the friction would be the last straw.

"We'll go eat. Shifting takes a lot of energy. I can see you're sapped," Trace remarked, turning and heading toward the kitchen.

Pearl bustled about the stove, an old dishtowel slung over one shoulder. She paused now and then to smooth gray flyaways back toward her otherwise neat, no-nonsense bun. She was dressed in a simple, long-sleeved white nightgown type thing, the collar maidenly high and stiff with starch. One imitation pearl button gleamed at the top, and when she turned to catch me staring, she flashed a wide, toothy grin.

The kitchen was full of cows. That's right. Cows.

Cow oven mitts, cartoony cow salt and pepper shakers… There was even a cow soap dispenser on the gleaming steel sink. The stove was an outdated tan, likely from the seventies, and I caught a faint whiff of gas as she fired up another burner, mumbling something about tea and how it's great for the bowels.

Aunt Mag ate mechanically, staring intensely into her plate as if the food might magically transform into a much-need Valium.

Oz sat to my right, chewing with pissed-off gusto, tearing into a chicken thigh and almost simultaneously shoving in a heaping spoonful of mashed potatoes. He leaned forward, staring at Trace who sat on the other side as Oz's jaw mashed the food furiously. I don't know what he was trying to convey. I wondered if he knew it was hard to look threatening with mashed potatoes on your upper lip.

The food was good, and I surprised myself by eating three crispy, tender deep-fried chicken breasts, two heaping helpings of mashed potatoes and three yeast rolls. After I was done I belched loudly, beyond mannerisms, and was swatted from behind with a dishtowel. I turned to find Pearl glaring.

"That's plum disrespectful. Let it loose anywhere but my kitchen. Didn't your mama teach you better than that?"

I was kind of concerned that she was going to grab me by the ear, bend me over her knee and send Trace to fetch a switch, but I managed to extract myself by ducking under her arm. I felt Trace watching my back and I shivered, as if I could physically shake off the weight of his gaze. I waited in the living room, feeling revived and full of nervous energy. I sat picking at a hangnail, and nearly jumped out of my skin when I raised my head. Pearl was standing directly in front of me, and I marveled at her stealth. I hadn't heard so much as a floorboard creak.

"I got somethin' for ya. Don't know how much good it'll do considerin' you're still not in control of your beast, but it can't hurt to give it to ya now, just in case."

She grasped a strange bracelet in her wrinkled hand that clicked as she held it out to me. I leaned in close, realized what it was made of and recoiled.

"Those look like bones," I told her, pressing my fingers to my lips.

"Yep," she nodded. "Sure are. Don't worry, they ain't human."

Like that was supposed to make a difference?

She sighed, and that lightning quick, liver-spotted hand shot out, grabbing my wrist. I gasped, "Ow!" as she squeezed, and my fist uncurled dutifully.

She dropped the bracelet into my palm, then closed it with her thin, gnarled fingers.

"It's a gift, ya brat. Seein' as you're new and all you'd better get used to it. All shifters wear these when they're transitioning. Them there are the bones of four different animals. The hawk, the grizzly, the rat and the snake. You can conjure up your panther at will, 'cause it's yours. It's part of you. But as you very well know you can also transform into other things...or in your case, *beings* — by touch. We'll talk about your new talent later, but for right now, take these. By having these bones in contact with your skin, you can transform into any of the critters I mentioned if you focus on 'em hard enough. I don't know how useful they'll be tonight, but on the off chance that things get unpleasant, with these you might have a shot at turnin' into somethin' that can hightail it and get out of harm's way."

I wordlessly opened my hand and gingerly picked up the bracelet. I slipped it on, feeling the rawhide string that ran through the tiny bones give just enough for me to slip it over my hand.

"I can...I can fly?" I whispered, feeling something that almost felt like giddiness jump into my throat.

"I reckon that's what hawks do." She smiled, her eyes twinkling mischievously.

My pulse quickened. I was at war with my panther, in love while in its form, and filled with dread when I wasn't.

I think what disturbed me most of all was how right it felt to be not human. On some dark, secret level, I was afraid, afraid that I would lose myself to the beast inside and that the girl with aqua eyes and chestnut hair would die, forever giving herself over to the wild thing that was always waiting, shoulders humped, ready to spring at any chance to escape.

But I had to admit, the possibility that I could become something with wings and actually fly was pretty damn cool. I felt curiosity not spawned by horror, but by wonder. My insides jumped in time with my pulse and I balled up my hands, offering Pearl the first genuine smile I'd given her.

She winked, turning and stepping lightly out of the room. A few moments later I could hear Aunt Mag speaking to Pearl in hushed, calm tones. When the boys filed through the hall, giving each other more than enough walking space, I sprang to my feet like the couch had bitten my butt.

I followed Trace, stopping to put my hand on Oz's chest. He halted at my touch- looking down into my face with his big brown eyes full of obvious concern.

"Um, Oz...I think this is where you should hang tight, okay? I want you to stay inside, all right?"

He opened his mouth to protest, but I spun on my heel, not missing the smug, victorious smile that Trace shot Oz as he opened the front door.

Chapter Twelve

Brewing Storm

When I stepped out onto the small, untreated porch I was almost literally pushed down by a mountainous wave of magic. I counted maybe thirty vampires. I could pick them out easily — it wasn't anything physical — although if I stared hard enough I could separate them by eye color. The shifters might as well have been singing to me — there was a scent, and a sense of shared kinship among the other shifters. Their animals called out, seeing a newcomer, and I could practically feel the vibration that went through them. I guess I expected them to dress in moth-eaten Victorian clothes, to play up the mystical being image, but all of them dressed modernly. A couple wore suits, a few were dressed casually — with one vampire sporting a black Metallica shirt. Some of them I could have mistaken for country club snobs. One vampire wore a bright blue polo shirt, and he tapped away on the Android in his hand, texting God only knew. I'll bet his Facebook posts were interesting. I don't know which was harder to believe, that the yard was crammed with a mix of at least thirty vampires and shifters, or that he was actually getting cell service on this mountaintop. But the most unsettling part of all? None of them looked a day over thirty. It was hard to take them seriously when the majority looked like frat boys.

"What's the plan?" I hissed from the corner of my mouth, never taking my eyes off the group of oddities who all seemed to glance up and study me at once.

"Very simple," Laylian replied, sounding chipper. "You

lead us to their den and we rush them. My clan is to hold them off and let the shifters do what they do best—turn them into dust." Then I realized that the group was indeed divided by kind. Something rippled occasionally over the crowd, and when I looked a little closer I saw that it was tension. The vampires and shifters were working together, and seemingly making the best of it, but I could see both sides struggling to keep their inner predators in check. I held my breath, waiting for someone to growl and break their eerie silence, for someone to throw the first punch, but they all stared straight ahead—straight at me.

I bit my lip, taking no comfort in the silence of the mass of brooding bodies in the yard. Three of them peeled away from the crowd and came to stand before Laylian, quiet, watchful, waiting for some cue.

One of them was a sharp-featured black man. His red eyes should have scared me but instead they lent him an exotic look. His head was slick and shaved and he was garbed in flowing white clothing that looked almost like pajamas. The other boy looked to be not a day over seventeen. His curly brown hair reminded me of sheep's wool with its springy, close-cropped curls. Wide, glowing red eyes appraised me and he smiled, showing twin sharp fangs. He wore blue-stone washed jeans and a wife-beater. He cracked the knuckles of his long, pianist fingers and nodded a hello. The third was a chick, and instantly I felt a pang of envy. Her long dark hair hung in silky, loose curls that reached the small of her back. She was tiny boned, delicate and exotic, and her sulking full pout screamed that she wasn't very happy about whatever orders she was about to receive. Big, brown eyes squinted at me, the black lashes so thick I wondered if they were real. A pea-sized beauty mark sat above her lip and just off to the right, perfectly positioned. Flawless, cinnamon skin was exposed by her tiny spaghetti tee and daisy dukes. I wanted to smack her, and I had no rational excuse for the urge.

Perfection kind of has that effect on me. I labeled her as

a bitch right there. I'd seen the look she'd burned my way on more than one female face in my time. She flipped her hair and it was a confirmation—she was vain, spoiled and would throw a major fit on anyone who dared tell her no. It was probably terrible of me, judging a book by its cover and all, but I really believe that females have a couple of extra senses—a built in bitch-o-meter, not to mention a whore-o-meter. If she'd had a cup of yogurt, she would have flung it in my hair.

Laylian smiled at each of them and I could see them practically purring, glowing with pleasure at the simple gesture their leader favored them with. "You three are some of the most clever we have, not to mention skilled. Tonight, as you know, your only goal will be to ensure that the new shifter remains safe. Should she suffer harm under your watch, you will lose my favor, and possibly your heads. Is that clear?"

My mouth dropped open in horror, because the threats rang true. He would actually kill them, just like that, if I got injured? I tried to push the thought away but it nagged me for some reason. Why did I care? It wasn't like they were human. They were unnatural, scary and...

And my mother was now one of them.

It was still a sore, nasty thought, and I actually flinched as I tried to put it on the back burner of my psyche, telling myself that I should pay attention, my life was at stake. Death was a possibility, and not just any death. I was pretty certain the vampires would rip me from limb from limb. I needed a clear head, which I knew wasn't possible. The best I could hope for was placing one foot in front of the other correctly and that I'd run when the time was right. I said a silent prayer of thanks that I was able to convince Oz to stay back with Aunt Mag and Pearl.

A giant, steel-gray Hummer sat idling in the gravel, and the attractive black vampire guy walked gracefully up to me and offered his arm.

His musical, husky Jamaican accent was gorgeous. "My

name is Jerico. It is a pleasure to be of service to you this night. I have heard wonderful things about you from our master. Will you please let me escort you to the vehicle? We will be driving. The others will follow behind."

"But…um, I see no other cars?" I slipped my arm cautiously into his, feeling awkward and sloppy in his presence but he smiled, and even though two twin sharp fangs dimpled his lower lip, it still somehow managed to look genuine. He was almost comforting. I could smell him, too. I would have expected him to smell like the demon I'd killed in the forest. I shivered, telling myself I could analyze the event later. I was still having trouble believing that had even happened. But yeah, the sharply handsome Jerico didn't smell like the demon, or like Laylian, instead he smelled… well, delicious. He smelled like cologne and something sweet. Flowers? Blueberries? It was hard to pinpoint. My panther didn't growl while he was near me, didn't struggle to break free when he placed one cold, gentle hand on the arm I had tucked through the crook of his elbow. The beast inside simply watched, waiting for its cue, and was not at all impressed.

"They have no need." He answered my question, his rich, musical voice reassured me, and a sea of red, glowing eyes all turned on us at once. I shivered, looking down, focusing on my footfalls and the quiet sound of Trace walking behind me, his sneakers making crunching noises on the gravel. Everyone stared. Jerico opened the back door of the Hummer, and I allowed him to give me a small boost with his hand under my forearm. I opened my mouth to thank him, feeling detached and dreamy with the surrealness of it all, but instead my eyes locked on Trace, who was talking animatedly with the gorgeous brunette vampire who had been glaring petulantly at me earlier.

Jerico cleared his throat politely. "I'll be in front of you for the drive. If you need anything, anything at all, please don't hesitate to tap on my shoulder."

I swear, even with fangs and looking not a day over

147

twenty-three, he emitted something fatherly. I wondered how a creature that drank the blood of the living and couldn't withstand sunlight could be charming. I nodded and he stepped back to shut the door. I craned my neck, watching as the pretty brunette grabbed Trace's arm, and I saw something passionate spark in her eyes as she dragged him away.

The back driver's side door swung wide and someone jumped in so fast they actually blurred. His scent filled the roomy cab like a burst of air freshener—clean linen and a baby powder smell. The curly-headed vampire in the wife-beater grinned as he settled in, red eyes dulled in the interior light to a pale pink.

"Hi, I'm Shane," he said simply, his voice high and young. Dimples appeared in his smooth white cheeks. "I'm super pumped about tonight. I've been training for three years for this. It's not every day a group of vampires goes rogue. I mean, you get the ones who go batshit, but they're usually solitaire. This is like, a small army. It's gonna be wicked."

I wrinkled my brow, and when he extended a slender, pianist's hand, I hesitated for just a moment before I placed mine in his. I expected a brisk pump of a handshake but instead he quickly flipped my hand palm down, curled my fingers under with his and raised my hand to his lips. I tried to yank it back, warning bells going off in my head, wondering if I'd been trapped wondering if he was gonna bite into the back of my hand like a ripe apple and rip off a chunk, veins and all—but instead he softly pressed his cold lips to it, releasing his grip immediately afterward. He laughed when I brought my hand to my chest, rubbing it as if it had been scalded.

"Jumpy?" he asked, his eyebrow quirking up.

"No. It's just…" I tried to think of a better word to describe my reaction, and failed miserably. "Shit."

"Yeah," he agreed, drumming his hands on his thighs to some beat I couldn't hear. "I mean, if I were gonna go ape and drain someone, it wouldn't be you. I like my women with a little extra…somethin'. You get what I'm saying?"

I guess vampires can get their pride wounded too. I probably deserved that, but it still stung.

"Oh? What's wrong? My pulse turns you off?" I couldn't resist.

But he just laughed as if I'd said the most amusing thing on the planet. "More like, a little thicker, a lot taller and with actual manners."

"So says the boy whose idea of a hot date is someone with his favorite blood type," I spat, looking down and doing a quick body check, suddenly painfully aware of my narrow hips and borderline C-cup.

Then my hearing perked up, catching a familiar, smart-ass voice. It was too muffled to make out, but I knew who the voice belonged to and had a pretty good idea of where it was coming from.

"I'll be right back, okay? I need to step out and check something." I didn't look at flirty wife-beater boy, and when he asked what I needed to check I ignored him, assuring him I'd only take a second.

I opened the Hummer's door as quietly as I could, leaving it open, and crept toward the back.

Trace stood with his right side profile in my view, his eyes closed. His strong, capable hands were on the brunette vampire's bare shoulders. Her small hands were in his hair and she pressed close, her pink tongue snaking out to touch his earlobe.

I couldn't help it. A choked sound ripped from my throat and I covered my mouth. Too late, both of their heads whipped around and the brunette smiled wickedly. It was the universal mean-girl smile. A smile meant to unravel my confidence, holding a promise of future emotional torture. Trace's mouth dropped open and his hands pushed at the brunette's shoulders, causing her to stumble in surprise.

"Wren? I thought you'd been settled in the ride," he said stiffly, eyes burning with obvious annoyance.

I turned on my heel, lifting my chin and making my way

back to the jutting door. I climbed up into the Hummer's backseat. A million emotions roiled and I felt a little nauseous. I was having trouble justifying my reaction, and my brain hurt as I tried to understand why I felt like I'd been punched in the gut. I pressed my lips together and didn't respond when Jackass Justin Timberlake asked me what had my 'panties in a wad'. Manners, indeed.

Two minutes later and my weird new shifter radar sounded as a burly, bearded shifter hopped into the driver's seat. "You just tell me where to go, miss. Take your time. I don't know how it works, but they said you'd be able to feel those bastards out. Name's Luke, by the way. Sorry as shit about your mama. She doctored my mommy once, fixed 'er right up. She'll be ninety-two this winter."

A local, and one who I recognized now that I really looked at him. He worked down at the hardware store, and had even come out to repair our broken dryer once when Mom's determined do-it-yourself methods had failed.

"Um. Thanks." I wondered if he knew that she wasn't sick anymore. Was he offering his condolences because of her cancer, or because she was now one of the undead? I really didn't want to know.

Instead I took out the small handkerchief Laylian had passed to me in the hall earlier and shut my eyes. The contact with the cloth on the pads of my fingers had an instant effect—it was like a string attached to my navel pulled taut.

"Go," I told the man in the driver's seat, feeling just a little safer with his presence.

He pushed the Hummer into gear, leading us down the bumpy mountainside that was a poor excuse for a driveway.

I let go of the cord, clamping down on my mental compass to look through the back window. My new improved shifter eyesight had no trouble slicing through the thick darkness and the windows' tint, and I gasped at the rolling wave of bodies behind us.

Vampires jogged, a small army, red eyes bouncing in the

shadows. Above them, numerous birds flew, some dipping close to the ground. Others glided lazily, following the Hummer's descent. I spotted an owl, snow-white in the moonlight, and several hawks. Others were plainer, tiny, but even with my superb new vision, I couldn't focus on the fine details.

It was an amazing sight and I shivered, thankful that I wasn't the one they were interested in snuffing out. Jerico sat in front of me, and he turned as we reached the bottom of the mountain, just a few feet from the smooth pavement of the main road. His red eyes stared into mine, waiting for a cue. The burly driver had turned in his seat, too, although he kept one hand on the steering wheel. I heard Shane stirring impatiently beside me. His restlessness screamed newbie, and the normal, annoying teenaged behavior comforted me in a way. I took a deep breath, nodded at Jerico, and shut my eyes. The invisible cord leading from my midsection pulled tighter this time around, as if I were a magnet drawing slowly closer to its mark. I could feel him, and I almost pulled away. I shivered, suddenly feeling dirty, like I'd bathed in warm pond scum.

"Left," I said with effort, resisting the urge to break the connection to the awful creature I'd seen in the tunnel during my vision at the cabin. I gripped the fabric harder, then suddenly I was no longer in the backseat of the Hummer, I was underground. I caught a glimpse of a pale, writhing body. Bound and gagged, her chest heaved. Dirty red hair spilled into her eyes and she made muffled, terrified sounds behind the overly tight gag that had split the corners of her lips, leaving a trail of dried blood on her chin. The man on the other side of the tunnel lay motionless, his hands unbound. His eyes stared sightlessly at the tied woman, his fingers clenched into eternal fists in front of him.

But yes, this time, something was different. I tasted vomit in my throat and a sob broke through. I felt a shift in the very air of the tunnel then I was zooming at breakneck speed through its length, screeching to a halt only to float

151

just beyond the bedside of the colorless beast. A thin, buxom blonde vampire lay with white limbs sprawled at his side, bare back exposed. She was smiling, looking like a cat that had just swiped the cream. He'd been toying with her blonde curls, letting them slip through his long-nailed fingers. I wondered how they'd managed to get an actual bed down here, and not only that. The bed looked super clean to be in a room made of packed grime. I zoomed out a bit, wishing I could control my movement and sort of expecting to see something that resembled a bedroom, but the rest of the room was earthen floors and walls. I remembered the woman tied up somewhere else, eyes wide and rolling with fear, the man I figured to be her husband mere feet in front of her, dead.

I sobbed again soundlessly. The albino vampire's head jerked up and he sprang naked from the bed, coma-white, tense, ready. A dingy bulb hung motionless from a cord on the dirt ceiling, dingy light illuminating his thin, wiry body as he circled the bed. He sniffed the air then relaxed, a slow smile creeping over his features, making the scar that ran from lip to ear dimple and stand out. The blonde vampire had flipped herself around and had bent at the waist on the bed, breasts covered by a thin sheet. She pouted, flipping her hair. Her eyes were fever bright as her hungry gaze ran over him, and I could smell her disgusting lust mingling with his own, though of a different kind.

"Come back to bed, *mon amour*. Are you finished with me so soon?" she asked prettily, licking her lips suggestively.

He raised his hand, halting her as she began to whine again, and a look of hurt flashed over her pretty painted face before she flounced back down on the bed, arranging her hair across the sheets so it would lie in a more flattering way.

"Little shifter," he whispered slowly, a touch of French and some other unidentifiable accent making the words almost impossible to understand. "Oh…" he said, genuine surprise making his red eyes flicker like two twin fires. He tilted his head back, looking up, then his eyes locked on me. I kicked, not able to see or control my legs. I felt like a giant stone, suspended cartoonishly in the air in that moment before I would plummet to the ground. He laughed, and I realized with relief that he wasn't making eye contact with me. Still, his gaze was stuck on the general area my spirit self was floating in. He sensed me, damn it. Somehow, he sensed me and knew what I was.

Yeah. That could be a problem. Would it somehow tip him off that there was a small army of shifters and vampires on their way to exterminate him? I pulled with all of my might, fighting to break free and make it back to my body. I struggled, feeling what could only be my soul shudder with fear and disgust for the white-haired, naked monster below me, and without warning I was slammed back into myself, opening my eyes and reaching out blindly, grasping the headrest of Jerico's seat. He had turned, craning his neck and looking at me with what could only be real concern.

"Where did you go, little one?" he asked, his beautiful voice an anchor. I stared into his glowing red eyes, finding strange comfort in their depths. When it came to all of the beasties I'd met recently, Jerico wasn't half bad. I shivered, hugging myself and looking over my shoulder. Every now and then a shadow would dart across the pavement behind us, or something would dip from the sky, gliding low only to soar out of view once again. We had to be doing at least fifty-five miles an hour, but I knew they were following. Their magic surrounded me, a mixture of the dangerous cunning of vampires and the barely restrained savagery of the shifters.

"The people," I whispered. "I think only one of them is alive. It's a woman. I think the others are…"

He nodded, his stare not wavering.

I focused on our target once again, hoping I wouldn't get sucked back into his creepy torture sex chamber. I didn't know what other horrors waited farther down the tunnel, and I really didn't want to find out. The invisible string pulled tight, making my stomach pitch and clench. We were on the right track. I rubbed the handkerchief between my fingers, wondering if the head rogue vampire had ever used it to dab an innocent victim's blood from the corner of his lips. I shuddered.

Ten minutes later, and we were reaching our destination. I told the burly driver to slow down and he braked softly. We were in a small community named Rowdy, although it wasn't as wild as the name suggested. Homes dotted the mountainside, porch lights shining, revealing roomy lawns and parked ATVs that were splattered with mud. The driver parked in a wide spot next to a curb that wound its way snake-like to the top. At the hill's crest was the entrance to what locals called Lost Mountain. The two lane highway we'd come in on divided the site, one side still being stripped and deep-mined, the opposite serving as a place to explore on ATVs, its mines abandoned and the land desert-like. Elk often frequented the area in large herds, almost as tame as cows they were so well protected by the local game wardens. The constant hum of dozers and various large machinery was a familiar sound heard on either side. Guards were posted on the operational side in white trucks, ready to ward off any ruffians who decided to sneak onto the mine site for shits and giggles, or for something more serious — like attempting to steal pieces of mining equipment worth thousands of dollars.

Jerico and the bearded man who had called himself Luke spoke in hushed tones. Shane was a jittery ball of energy beside of me, causing the seat to squeak as he leaned forward, trying to get in on whatever the two men in front were discussing.

I let the link die, exhaling in relief as I dropped the white hanky onto my shorts. I felt like I'd just done an intense abdominal workout from the tension I'd held in my muscles while I'd guided us to the area where the awful vampire leader was hiding with his followers.

I jumped as someone tapped on my side of the Hummer,

then suddenly the door was yanked unceremoniously open. Trace frowned in, the brunette vampire girl sulking behind him and fixing me with a chilly stare. I gave them both a look meant to convey my annoyance. "Where's Laylian?"

"He's busy with final preparations," the vampire girl said softly, her voice velvety and smooth, sounding far more mature than my own. Great. Not only was she drop-dead gorgeous, she also had the voice of a phone-sex operator. Something sank its claws deep into my gut and twisted, and I felt the overpowering desire to say something awful, to insult her in some way. I realized I wanted to piss her off grandly because...

Because, because... Why?

I didn't understand. Nope. Not a bit. But if I was honest with myself, all of the weird feelings combined could be summed up in one word—jealousy. I'd seen her pressed against Trace, and it had made me jealous. Furiously jealous. Rip-her-hair-out jealous. As if reading my ridiculous thoughts, she stepped forward, hooking her arm through Trace's, resting her head against his arm. She smiled, and to the untrained eye the smile might have been considered friendly, but I saw it for what it was. Smug. Why was she so obviously trying to mark her territory? Why now, of all times? Why did I even give a shit? I felt the warning tingle of the shift and pushed it back. No. I would not get furry now.

If the twit thought she could spazz me out that easily, she had another thing coming. I realized my hands were balled into fists and with effort made them relax. I let my shoulders roll back, lifted my chin, and gave her a sickly sweet smile of my own.

"Thank you. I really appreciate you agreeing to help me tonight. What's your name, by the way? I don't think I caught it earlier."

She was taken aback by my kindness, and I felt my own smug satisfaction threatening to spill out and run over my expression in the form of a satisfied grin. I pushed it back, savoring the warm success deep inside. Trace didn't appear to be interested in either of us, and was instead looking to his left, scanning the winding road leading to the entrance of our destination.

"Michelle," she said uncertainly, squinting her big, long-lashed expressive red eyes and cocking her head to the side. I felt something probing gently at my mind, trying to flip my thoughts over and see the motive beneath and I clamped down, somehow knowing just what to do with what I can only guess was shifter instinct. I envisioned a brick wall guarding my thoughts. The fingers curling around my secret desires tossed them down, yanking back as if scalded. Michelle gasped softly and swayed on her feet, composing herself so quickly I wouldn't have noticed had I not been looking for some type of reaction.

Great. Just great. I guess that's another perk to being one of the undead. I shivered, thinking of Mom. She'd pried into my business enough while she'd been human. If I ever got the chance to be around her again, would she try to use her vampire voodoo to pry into my private thoughts? The thought made me want to vomit, and I decided that I'd worry about that if and when the time came.

The important thing was that I'd effectively pushed her out. What else were the vampires capable of? If they could slip into your head and pick apart your innermost desires, could they also secretly influence them as well? I had so many questions. Questions about what I was, what I was capable of and just what I was up against.

I swung my legs out, almost kicking Trace in the gut, and wedged between him and Michelle. She smelled like lilac and surprisingly powerful magic, and the new sixth sense inside told me that for all of her girly dramatics, she was old, really old.

I needed a joint, a beer and a boy with hard abs telling me how much he liked me. I needed to lose myself in mindless, empty enjoyment and short-lived satisfaction. I wasn't cut out for saving the town. Heck, I wasn't even cut out for saving myself. I was a stoner, a virgin tease, a bad girl. I wasn't a leader. Someone had gotten my destiny all wrong.

When I looked behind the Hummer, my jaw dropped. The large group of vampires stood almost completely motionless. Some of them wore guns slung across their backs while others had sheathed swords on their hips. A couple held wicked-looking knives in their hands. One of them was quietly checking his compact bow, red tipped arrows in a sheath on his back.

If someone drove by, Perry County would be roaring with gossip for weeks, not to mention everyone and everyone's mama would be 'callin' the law'.

But that wasn't the cause of the stupid look on my face. Animals were everywhere. A few birds still remained, most of them owls or hawks, but the diversity was astounding. It was like a zoo had exploded there in the tiny community of Rowdy. A rabbit thumped by at by at breakneck speed and I hopped out of the way, sparing it a moment's glance. A lion stepped into view, and for a second my brain tried to rationalize why a lion was in the mountains of Perry County, Kentucky. Its human-blue eyes were trained on me, and my vision zoomed in on the irises. It shook its great mane, made a strange, crackly guffawing noise and sauntered by a black bear, glancing toward it long enough to emit a short, throaty purr that was so deep it seemed to vibrate in my teeth.

A small, red fox weaved in-between the crowd's feet, lightning quick and scampering lightly over the tips of the boots of several vampires. The vampires shifted uneasily, looking over their shoulders as if they expected to be turned to dust at any moment with the quick bite of a grumpy shifter. The fox yapped like a lapdog, its puffy red tail swishing around its dainty white feet. It sniffed the air, padded quickly toward the black bear, and pressed its tiny, cute button nose against the fur of the bear's thick leg.

Instantly the fox grew in height, length and weight, becoming a perfect clone of the brown bear. The former fox

157

grunted in what sounded like satisfaction, plopping down again a little closer to the pavement.

A cheetah sat hunkered close to the mountainside, tail swishing, sloped head twitching as if it could hear something the others couldn't. I saw everything from your normal domestic cat to a trio of hyenas making soft, strange laughing noises as they nipped at and sniffed one another.

It was all too much.

Only two of the shifters in the group were in human form, a pair of females I'd never seen before, and they stood naked, looking completely at ease and chatting with each other. I looked away, my face growing red. I had been wondering why more of them weren't in human form, and now remembered that they all must have shed their clothing back at the cabin when they'd shifted into different species of birds to keep up with the amazing speed of the vampires who'd run effortlessly behind the Hummer as we'd driven the speed limit on scenic Highway 15. I guess some of them weren't as comfortable as the two shapely females with letting it all hang out.

Someone was bound to come driving up the mountain at any moment, and I wondered if I should remind them of that. Surely they'd hear an approaching vehicle, right? Being seen by any humans at this point could spell disaster.

The tension in my body must have been noticeable, because I felt a cool hand on the small of my back. I turned, looking up into Laylian's red, almond-shaped eyes. His close-cropped red hair was vivid even in the darkness and his pale, creamy complexion gave me a moment of skin envy.

"If you're concerned about our privacy...no one can see us. Even if a busload of people were looking directly at this area, they'd see nothing but the usual. Pearl is very useful. She cast a cloaking spell before our departure. It should hold up through the night."

"So?" I asked, trying to hide my surprise. "Does this mean the other vampires can't see us? That's good, right?"

158

He shook his head. "It was designed to fool humans. It's a species-based spell, very specific."

I nodded stiffly, giving up on trying to wrap my head around that information. In the meantime, Laylian continued to stare at me expectantly, and I shook my head as if waking from a daze.

"Oh. Yeah. Okay… I'm ready if you are," I said awkwardly, not really looking forward to leading a small supernatural army to a den of bloodsucking whack jobs. "But, um, there's something you should know. When we made it to the main road earlier, while I was trying to track the albino dude, I was kinda transported into the tunnel again."

Laylian's expectant expression didn't change, but he slipped up a bit in his perfect composure, shifting his weight from one foot to the other and smoothing down the front of a black T-shirt he hadn't been wearing earlier. He cleared his throat, signaling me to go on.

I pushed my unruly hair back from my face, taking in a deep breath, smelling wild roses and pine. "Yeah. I saw the missing…married couple. The man was dead. The woman was alive, but she looked pretty rough. They're all staying in an abandoned mining tunnel. The…vampire was with another one, a female, and they were in a bed. Some of the others were just kinda lounging around."

He nodded, his eyes burning a brighter red for just a moment. "And?"

"He somehow knew I was there. He couldn't see me, not exactly, but he knew that I was watching somehow. He kept looking up. He spoke to me…he called me shifter. The woman he's holding captive was really, really scared."

A muscle in Laylian's jaw twitched. "Let me guess," he began, his tone careful and controlled. "You believe that your presence might have made him suspicious."

"Yeah," I said. "I mean, I'm not sure, but I get the feeling that they're gonna be watching things a little closer now."

Laylian shut his eyes for a moment, and in a very human gesture reached to massage his eyelids with the pads of his fingers.

"That's simply delightful, Wren. Intentionally or not, you've probably given him reason to be on alert. Now we have no idea what we may be walking into. This could very well jeopardize the entire operation. To my knowledge, Brass believed that we lost his trail long ago. We were falsely tipped off that they were hiding somewhere across the Mexican border, but luckily he has a very real weakness — women. A female of our clan has been keeping in contact with him for the past two weeks. He willingly told her which city they were planning to dominate, but not the exact location. She's convinced him that we're still overturning every rock in Mexico in our search but now…."

"What Laylian is trying to say," a now-familiar voice interjected with false cheer, "is that you unintentionally screwed everything up. Nice job, Wren. Your first night on the job has been a raging success."

I whirled on Trace. "This is not my damn job. And how the hell was I supposed to know that he could tell I was there? It's not like I know how this tracker stuff works. You seem to forget that less than three nights ago I didn't even know this…this craziness existed. Remember, you're the one who got me into this mess to begin with. If you would have just left me alone…"

"You'd have been a midnight snack. Now shut up before you wake the trolls."

I took the bait and looked around frantically in search of some hideous new wonder, and thought about just hiding out in the Hummer and letting them all search out the vampire den by themselves.

I needed Oz. Oz and an alcoholic beverage with a side of elephant tranquilizer. I was ready to throw my hands up and tell Laylian he was on his own, deal or not, but then Michelle seemingly materialized out of thin air to stand close to Trace, one tan, perfectly toned arm snaking around his waist. She sensed my weakness, and the satisfied whisper of a smirk on her heart-shaped face made me plant my feet a little deeper into bits of asphalt that had broken from the side of the road. I felt a tap on my shoulder, hesitant, light as a butterfly, and turned to stare down at a girl who looked fourteen at most. Her razored, short black hair was styled into pointy tips that shimmered with gel in the moonlight. Her large hazel eyes dominated her round-cheeked, cherubic face. She dropped her gaze and slowly held something out to me. I looked down and saw a pair of jeans and a black T-shirt. Embarrassment burned my cheeks at the sight of my bare legs, oversized shorts used for lounging around the house reaching my knees. My tee swallowed me too, hanging almost mid-thigh. I could feel everyone's eyes one me and I groaned. I was ready to lead them all into battle wearing my makeshift pajamas.

After I'd shimmied into the jeans in the comforting, quiet darkness of the Hummer, and slipped into the comfortable, waist-length black tee, I emerged and started walking uphill, not sparing a glance behind me. I held the hanky loosely in my hand, resisting the urge to toss it down. Just holding it made me feel filthy and gave me the urge to soak my hand in a gallon bucket of bleach until it wrinkled up like it did if I soaked in the tub for too long.

I sent out my invisible cord, feeling my stomach tighten and ache. I only held on to it for a moment to make sure our target was still in the underground mine, then shook it off, unable to keep myself from rubbing my arms in an attempt to smooth the chill bumps that covered them from the disturbing contact.

The group was amazingly silent and I looked behind once, making sure I wasn't walking alone. I almost shrieked when I saw one of the lumbering brown bears directly behind me. A vampire stepped lightly to his left, red eyes looking straight ahead. He kept a safe distance from the bear, and I didn't blame him. There were forty vamps and only around eleven shifters, but the vamps didn't seem to feel very safe even against those odds. I guess my kind had a pretty terrifying reputation, being the assassins of the

161

supernatural world and all. I wondered what would happen if one shifter attacked one of the vampires. Would they all follow suit? For now the group was almost in perfect single file, sticking to the edge of the pavement on the outside edge of the two-lane road. The climb was one giant, sharp curve with no shoulder. The curb was treacherous, and had caused many a driver to crash when taken too quickly. With my new and surprisingly awesome night vision, I could peer over the edge into the kudzu vines that covered the steep, gently slanting drop. I could see rusted car doors and dirty, faded tires twisted in the crowded trees at the bottom. I shuddered, glad that my brakes had never gone out in this particular curb.

But that was south-eastern Kentucky for you. For many of us, our first rides home after being delivered kicking and screaming at our local, modest hospital were through these very hills. Straight stretches were a rarity, and dodging roadkill was an everyday occurrence. A month ago a hot senior named Simon had dodged a doe crossing the road with her fawn after we'd done some heavy making out on Lost Mountain and had nearly sent us over the edge. I'd almost peed myself, and had made up my mind that I'd never ride with him again. I'm all for preserving our wildlife, but I didn't want to meet my maker due to Bambi and his mom.

I paused at the wide mouth of the rocky road that led onto the strip job, and wondered where my mother was, and what she was doing. Was she being educated on vampire etiquette? Was she locked inside an empty room, crying out my name? Was she sipping a blood martini? I tried not to think about it. I tried to push thoughts of her to the back of my mind, reminding myself that my survival was at stake. I'd deal with my mama drama later—I'd curl up in my warm, safe bed and let everything sink in.

I'd probably go crazy when, and if, I ever had time to reflect. I was already halfway convinced that this was some sort of bad dream and that I was simply playing it out like an actress as I drooled on my pillow in my soft, oversized PJs.

By the time we'd made it to the very top of the twisting, sinuous mountain, I'd expected my legs to ache, but they didn't. Normally I would have at least been breathing a little faster, but my breathing was steady, relaxed. I felt weirdly energized. My scalp tingled, my panther itching to show itself as we made our way slowly closer to our destination. I heard one of the shifters growl behind me and the hair on my neck rose in response. I had to physically shake myself to keep my body from shifting and I ached deep inside my gut. I imagined it was what an ex-alcoholic felt like when they passed a bar with drunken laughter bellowing from inside. The other shifters called to me, even if they weren't intentionally doing so. Their magic smelled like ambrosia, and the unintentional peer pressure made my legs quiver.

I stalled, not looking back, letting the invisible cord tug at my navel, feeling out the location of the horrible black souls that would soon be extinct if the attack was successful. Common sense told me I was in way too deep. Logic told me I was a babe in the woods, and that I would most likely die a horrible, gut-spurting death. But I couldn't call it quits now. Too much was on the line. Besides, if I backed out now, what would happen to my mother? Laylian seemed pretty cool for a bloodsucking, unnatural creature, but how nice would he be if I bailed? I shivered at the thought, not planning on finding out.

I almost whirled, feeling hot breath on my neck, but the scent of the body behind me was all I needed to confirm the identity, and I took an odd comfort in Trace's nearness.

"Are you just gonna stand here, or are we gonna get this over with? I'd like to get back to the cabin and finish off the leftover fried chicken, if that weakling you're so protective over hasn't finished it off."

Charming as all hell.

I couldn't help myself, I turned around. The black bear behind and to the left of Trace grunted and shifted from

163

foot to foot impatiently. The black-haired, red-eyed vampire beside him took a step to the side, keeping his hand on the hilt of long, sheathed sword with red rubies on its handle that glinted in the moonlight. Trace stood smug and shirtless, his jeans so low that I could see the waistband of his boxers. I tried to keep my eyes away from his abs, honest to God I did, but my eyes went there as if drawn magnetically. I tore my gaze away and met his glinting green eyes. Black lashes cast tiny shadows on his cheeks as he glared, and tiny pieces of hair curled against his cheek. I had the urge to reach out and push them away, threading them through my fingers as I did so, and immediately felt like an idiot. My body was tingling again, but not with the shift. No, it was tingling at the nearness of him, urging me to step closer to his heat. I felt my cheeks burning and a skittering spike of humiliation ran down my spine. I wondered if he could see my inner struggle playing across my face, or if he was could smell my attraction with his shifter senses. What came out of my mouth next sounded jealous even to me.

"Oh, did you put it in your pants long enough to break away from Michelle? And who are you anyway? Laylian is the one I owe a favor, not you—and that means you have no say over anything about this...this mission."

He laughed, and I wanted to claw his flawless olive face. When he spoke, his voice was so low that even my new sensitive hearing had trouble picking up his words. "Mission? Wow. This is really going to your head, isn't it? Don't you get it? They don't give a fuck about you. You're just a tool, a way to smoke out the hive. You think Laylian really cares if you make it through this alive tonight? Oh, precious...you've so much to learn. He's a bloodsucker. A very rich one. And even if I lend my...expertise to him at times, I never forget that. You'd do well to keep that in mind. Right now, you're useful, and you're fascinating to him with your particular talents, but don't mistake that for fondness. Vampires don't love. Remember that."

Oh, that stung. His words hit home, and two things happened — my face reddened with outrage, and my eyes filled with tears. Sure, his mocking pissed me off, but that wasn't what rubbed me so roughly. He'd said that vampires didn't love. My mother was now a vampire, and I felt like hyperventilating when I considered that she might be soulless — loveless. It was too horrible to contemplate.

I watched his face change as he watched my own fall. The annoyance was gone as if it had been smeared away by the world's fastest paintbrush, then he was reaching out, touching my arm almost hesitantly, something like concern scrunching his brow and softening the previously hard line of his full lips.

I jumped away as if his touch might burn me and focused on the almost perfect line of shifters and vampires behind us. The cheetah sauntered up from behind the black bear, stopping maybe a foot from my feet and slowly sitting down. Its human-brown eyes met my own, and its head bent just a little, ears lying flat. I smelled its magic, and I felt the rumbling in my chest again. Was I being challenged? I shook off the tingle, breathed in deep through my nose and surprised myself by smiling down at the large, exotic cat.

"Okay," I said, so lowly that I wasn't sure anyone could hear besides myself. "It's not much farther. I kind of have an idea of where the location is. Some friends and I once had a bonfire there. From here on out, we'll need to be quiet. We're getting pretty close."

I looked up at the sky, the stars burning bright the way they only did in Perry County. I sent a small plea to God that the woman with red hair was still alive. Though she was older than me, the fear in her eyes had given her a vulnerability that reminded me of a small child and tugged at my heart-strings. What must she be feeling now?

My voice sounded small and uncertain and I stuffed my hands into the pockets of my borrowed jeans that belonged to God-knows-who. I could feel Trace's eyes burning on my face and I looked behind me into the sprawling, rolling dozed-over hills that were mostly used for ATV explorations and by dirt bike enthusiasts. Then Laylian was standing beside me in the spot that had been empty two seconds before. I gasped, unable to keep myself from taking a step back. He cocked his head and those glowing red eyes bored into mine. A smile tugged at the corner of his lips. His hand reached out, grabbed a lock of my hair, and he let it slip easily through his pale fingers. "Your coloring is different, but you remind me so much of her. I'm sure she'd be proud of your bravery tonight."

I opened my mouth to pump him for details on my mother. Was she angry? Did she miss me?

Instead I turned and nodded toward the road. "Let's go. I'm ready to get this over with." Then I turned to meet his eyes once more. "After this I'm free and clear, right? After this, we've both held up our side of the bargain."

He nodded, grinned, then pushed me forward gently with his palm on the small of my back. He was getting a bit too comfortable with his hands, and later I would tell him just how much that annoyed me and creeped me out, but I could feel evil vibrating through the air. Heck, I could even smell it. I was guessing that it wouldn't be long before they sensed us too.

Chapter Thirteen

Chaos and Light

A cloud passed over the moon and obscured all but its particularly bright bow, darkening our path and seeming to mute the chirping of the crickets with the sudden absence of light. Michelle and Jerico had made their way to the front, with Michelle turning back occasionally to pierce me with an icy red glare. Jerico was stiff and alert, his muscled shoulders bunched under his shirt. The hilts of two leather-bound daggers jutted from his hips, held in place by an intricate black utility belt. Shane walked behind me, silent, bobbing his head to some unheard beat. A walk in the park, right? All he was missing were the earbuds and track pants. Laylian had asked Trace to guard the back of the group, but he'd stubbornly placed himself closer to my side. I kept stealing little glances to my left, trying not to notice how the shadows did nothing to obscure his beauty. He still didn't wear a shirt, and I wondered if that was for his personal comfort or for my personal torture.

I felt loud, like an elephant crashing through undergrowth as my feet knocked gravel and bits of trash left by riders. I attempted to be as silent as possible, but try as I might, I couldn't match the eerie, unnatural stealth of the group. Sure, I was probably a bit quieter than I would have been say, four nights ago. My steps had acquired a certain grace, but I was still a grasshopper in the supernatural world, and I obviously had a lot to learn.

I wished I didn't have to learn *anything* about this new world. Going back to the ignorant, sad stoner was starting to seem really attractive. I thought of Oz and my chest squeezed. The look in his eyes when I'd asked him to stay had sent a shard of guilt into my heart, and I told myself that it was for the best. But the selfish part of me wished that I'd dragged him along.

We walked downhill, and the bare, looming hills reminded me oddly of a desert. A whippoorwill sounded close by and the call echoed hollowly off the steep, man-made inclines. Lost Mountain was oddly silent, with traffic even being light on the highway maybe one hundred yards behind us. On a warm, balmy night such as this, there should have been at least a few late-night riders or partiers on the mountain. We should have smelled the smoke of a bonfire, or heard the echo of hardy laughter from someone with one shot of Jack too many, but it was as if the evil that lurked close by had radiated some type of repellant. Rabbits should have been dashing across the dusty, rocky road, startled by our passing, but I didn't see even one.

Then, all at once, oh man, I had to pee so bad.

The line that had been behind me had unraveled into a mass of assorted animals and the alert, glowing eyes of the vampires. I came to a sudden stop, clearing my throat and motioning to Laylian, who was leading the group behind me. He was easy to pick out, because everyone kept at least a few feet away from him, at a respectable distance. I could see his upper lip lift in the darkness in what was probably a snarl, but he walked forward, hands on hips. He dipped his chin to his chest, met my eyes, and waited.

"I....uh...I have to go. Um. I need to pee, really bad." I shuffled my feet, feeling my face burn, knowing that everyone in the group could probably easily hear me.

"Nice," Trace whispered from my side. "We're in the middle of an ambush, and you have to take a leak. May I compliment you on your awesome leadership skills? Can I call you Sergeant? Betty Badass, maybe?"

Laylian shot him a dark look, opened his mouth as if to protest, then let his shoulders slump.

"You may. But Michelle goes with you."

"No way!" I tried to fit as much displeasure as possible into my whisper. "I'm just gonna step over the hill here. I could feel them if there were any this close. And so could you, right?"

For the first time, I could tell that he was seriously losing his patience. Laylian's eye twitched, fangs peeped and pressed against his lower lip and his red hair seemed to glow with annoyance.

"Make it quick. Trace, go with her, keep a distance."

I was going to protest but I was about two seconds from doing the pee-pee dance. I set off down the small hill, almost sliding its length on my butt. Trace reached the bottom where the incline smoothed out into a tiny piece of land. I looked around and remembered where I was. This was an unfinished project from long ago—a shallow sediment pond created to catch runoff from heavy rains on mining sites after the mountain had been stripped of its trees. This one was far from finished. We hadn't had any rain in a while, and were on the verge of a drought, but I could tell that some aquatic animals had lived there not long ago from the dried frog carcasses littering the earth. Sparse, young grass was in patches on the bottom, the mud that had likely been thick a couple of weeks before had been fried to maplike cracks in the earth. "Turn your back, please." I tried to make my voice sound as chilly as possible, but I was already spooked from the shallow, empty enclosure. I was shuffling to the far end, my hands hesitantly prying at the button on my jeans. I was looking heavenward, praying the moon stayed hidden behind the puffy, massive cloud so my bare ass would have as much shadow as possible when Trace yanked me back.

"Watch your step!" he growled, keeping his voice low. I looked down, expecting a rattlesnake or a rabid raccoon. But I would have been even less surprised to see a crouching yeti taking a dump at my feet than what showed below me.

A ring of brown, plump mushrooms hunkered and

169

bowed below me. I'd seen them form in perfect circles before, but this time it was different. The cloud chose that moment to slide away from the room, illuminating the tiny, weird scene before me. Amazingly tiny, thumb-sized forms dashed around in the circle, but all of them pulled together before my eyes into the center, tiny, fair heads tilting up to stare at me. They were all blond, and were wearing what looked like woven leaves and bits of flowers as clothing. They glowed a bright blue color, and as I watched their combined light blazed and grew, becoming a large orb of light.

An angry buzzing noise assaulted my ears and I stepped back farther.

"Pixies," Trace whispered, his voice breathless, and if I didn't know better, a little scared. "Looks like you almost desecrated the fairy ring."

"Fairy ring?" I asked, turning, preparing to run while keeping my eyes glued to the now pulsating orb of blue light. "But I've seen those mushrooms before. There's no such thing as..."

"You had your human goggles on before, Wren. Apologize...now. We may be quick, but they're quicker. Apologize."

Then he was tugging the small mood ring my grandma had given me when I was five, when she'd began to get really sick, from my index finger. I'd worn it around my neck on a small chain until it had fit me properly. I loved it.

I attempted to pry his hand away, all while trying to get as far away from the small, glowing creatures as possible.

"What are you doing? Let's get out of here! If I interrupted them, I'm sorry. But we need to go."

"They're angry. We're in the middle of an ambush. We don't need angry faeries on our backs tonight too, Wren. You need to offer this as a gift." He popped the ring from my finger, the flesh stinging where the old silver had roughly grazed my knuckle.

"But my gran..."

He shushed me by placing his finger to my lips. One look at his wide green eyes and I agreed. He was scared, and I knew that if he was nervous, I should be too.

He handed the ring back, tucking it into my palm and closing my shaking fingers over it.

"Apologize and offer your gift. Be careful. Don't touch the mushrooms. They were dancing and they view the ring as sacred. You harm anything in that circle and we will both die."

Just great.

"But they're so…"

"Small?" he finished for me. "Pretty? Trust me on this one, have I lied to you yet?"

I thought about the fact that he'd spied on me for weeks. That didn't exactly strike me as honest.

He sighed, and the orb in the center of the ring of mushrooms grew from maybe cantaloupe-sized to volleyball-sized. The buzzing grew louder. None of the tiny, luminous creatures were visible now, just that bright, blazing orb of light. I could feel the heat of it on my skin as if were a small sun.

I had to strain to hear him. "They're small, Wren, but they pack more of a punch than anything you've come in contact with so far. We're not immune to their magic. I haven't pissed off a pixie in going on thirty years and I do not want to do it again."

I searched his face and he nodded. I bent down, not caring if I was getting my knees filthy with dusty earth. I crawled slowly forward, careful not to lose the ring, and almost stopped when the bright orb turned back into a dozen tiny, blue-glowing people. Most of them were female, I could see. But a few of the tiny men with leaves covering their middles flew forward on gauzy wings that cast silver glitter on the ground. A female soon followed, a tiny buttercup perched upon her blonde head. She landed just outside the ring and regarded me with silver-blue eyes.

I lay flat, not giving a shit how pathetic I must look to

Trace, who stayed back, and stretched my balled fist forward, palm up. I opened it up and the black stone in the mood ring reflected her bright, shimmering light.

"A gift," I said, my voice small, hardly a thready whisper. "I didn't mean to intrude. I hope you'll accept my apology."

At first she didn't move, and my body began to hum with the beginnings of the shift. But this time the panther inside didn't get angry. It wanted to get me the hell away. It was panicking. I pushed it back, my breath coming so hard that it blew tiny dust fragments around my face. God, they were so tiny, but I could feel their malevolence like rain, pelting my body with cool, wicked intent.

She stepped forward and the little men behind her in the ring made to follow. I could hear voices, too faint to understand, like the soft buzzing of insects or the beating of birds' wings. She held up one tiny, pale hand and they stayed put. She was obviously their leader.

She flew, silver glitter leaving a sparkling trail behind her. My breath caught at the beauty of the tiny creature. It was all so fairy-tale like that I could almost be lulled into thinking they were harmless if not for the icy protectiveness that billowed from the ring.

She landed in my hand and I almost jumped. I felt warm heat spreading through my fingers, and her weight was like that of a butterfly.

She bent, inspecting the ring with wide eyes, turning it over easily despite her size. She nodded as if satisfied, then she sprang toward my face, glitter and blue light blinding me for a moment. I almost swatted her away, prepared to run, but instead she hovered there in front of my nose.

Oh, she was the most lovely thing I'd ever seen. Her tiny features were perfection, like those of a porcelain doll. Glossy blonde curls spilled over her bare shoulders. Her leaf-like dress was tight on a waif thin body with her tiny feet dangling loosely in the air. Her wings beat so quickly I couldn't get a good look at them, throwing glitter in every direction. Then, ever so slowly, she hovered closer to my cheek and gave it a quick, light kiss. A feeling of peace came over me then, and my mouth gaped open in wonder. I felt calm, almost drunk with serenity. I could have curled up there beside of the ring of mushrooms and fallen into an effortless sleep. I felt so safe.

Trace didn't make a sound as several pixie women came forward and lifted the ring as a group effort. They carried it to the center of the ring and the leader followed. Soon they were blazing blue again, flitting in-between the mushrooms in a sparkling, twirling dance. Tiny bodies moved gracefully, spinning and spinning to music I couldn't hear. Celebrating nature. Celebrating life. My ring was in the center, and I thought that if I had to lose it, this was by far the coolest way.

And I really don't think Grandma would have minded.

After backing slowly away and leaving the pixies to dance, I numbly made my way back to the group. I could only stare wide-eyed at Laylian with dirty palms when Trace told him my break had been cut short.

He literally leaned in and sniffed me. "I smell Fae," he whispered, and actually took a step back.

"Yeah, well…I think my bathroom break can wait. Please. I'd rather not explain this right now." I told him, taking my place behind Michelle and Jerico once more. I was aware of Trace's hand on the small of my back. He kept darting concerned glances my way as we climbed a well-used ATV trail to the top of one rolling hill. An owl swooped by my head and I ducked instinctively as a brown feather broke free of its wing and lightly brushed my nose with its smoothness before it floated idly away on the lazy breeze.

I stretched out the invisible cord again, planning on making quick contact to assure myself the enemies hadn't left for a late-night abduction of some helpless human. I could still feel him close by, but until that moment I had somehow managed to avoid actually seeing him. I didn't know how I could control it, but I wished that I could get a visual. I wanted to make sure we weren't marching in

173

only to surprise them as they were leaving. I wanted to make sure they weren't somehow prepared for our arrival. I shut my eyes and willed my mind to follow the pull of evil nestled beneath the earth. An uncomfortable pang shot through my stomach and I was helplessly overcome with emotions I instinctively knew weren't my own. My inner GPS hit a brick wall, and I was aware of something pushing me back. I could almost feel the sting of nails on the pale, cold hand that it belonged to, and I flinched back, letting the connection fall.

The vampires knew we were here. They had known all along, and were much closer than I'd thought. Oh God, how could I not have known? But it wasn't like I was pro at this tracking stuff.

I was turning to shout to the group that the plan had changed, to ready their weapons or their fangs or whatever the hell they had that made them a formidable opponent against criminal vampires, but it was too late.

I heard something whistling through the air, and had I still been a slow, perfectly abnormally normal teenager, I would have taken a nice crack to the noggin, but instead I leaned back, seeing a blur pass in front of my face not five inches from my nose.

I looked to Trace, and I wanted to let the seductive rumble in my chest and the tingle in my scalp take me as far as it wished. I could feel his beast, too, responding to my own, and something rolled off him in a giant wave that almost made me forget that we were most likely about to die. For the first time I noticed that the locket he'd been wearing about his neck earlier that night was gone, and for some reason that bothered me a little. Protectiveness enveloped me, and it wasn't my own—it was Trace's.

I took a breath, intending to call out to Laylian, but all that came out was a roar. My shift was quicker this time and I transformed in two seconds flat, feeling my body pitch forward and my wide paws slap the earth. I kicked my way out of the clothes that had covered my human body and let go of the last traces of human reservations. Trace followed, dropping and almost seeming to flicker into full wolf form. The moonlight caught the luminous sheen of his fur and he shook his head as if ridding himself of the quickly fading tingles of the shift that danced across my own skull.

No one had to tell Laylian that something had gone horribly, catastrophically wrong. He was shouting orders and commanding the group to get ready as I crept closer to Trace's side. It was the first time we'd been in our animal forms together, but instead of feeling challenged, my panther felt safer, stronger, at his side.

Trace was growling and I saw him look up, one paw stamping the dry earth. Something soared in the air above my head, a hawk circling. Its warning cry carried as if from surround-sound speakers into the eerily silent night.

I summoned the anger that had been simmering for the past few months, and now that I looked back, I knew it wasn't just the stress and my mother's condition that had kept me on edge and sharpened my tongue enough to cut everyone near me with my harsh words. It had been the panther wrestling for acknowledgment. It had been my destiny crying out to be fulfilled.

And as the first wave of them closed in around us I didn't question who I was or what my purpose was, because I knew. I was a shifter, and this was what I'd been created for. As I pulled my lips away from my fangs and hunkered low, ears back, tail low, shoulders bunched and hindquarters trembling, ready to spring, some missing part of me that had been bouncing around for as long as I could remember suddenly clicked back into its rightful place.

The panther roared, and it wasn't just a battle cry, but a testament. A new creature was born and I handed over the reins to the beast. The enemies were all dressed in black, and their weapons were primal at best. Crowbars, metal baseball bats, even handguns clashed with the graceful arcs' of my group's blades and flying arrows. I watched as a grizzly lifted its jiggling bulk to stand on its back feet.

175

A small female vampire in a tattered black dress sprang it its direction, fangs bared, dark hair snaking around her face like curls of smoke. She'd misjudged her distance in the chaos, and with one lightning quick swipe of a massive paw the bear sent her head rolling grotesquely from her shoulders. She was turned to dust, coating the animal's fur in gray as the cloud that had once been flesh puffed around its massive form.

Something slammed into me from the side and I rolled a few feet, catching a glimpse of Trace sinking his jagged teeth into the thigh of a thin, gangly vampire. Something screamed with rage and I looked up, seeing the face of my new opponent. Red, blazing eyes burned in a haggard, older face. His gray hair was a puff of springy, frizzy curls and his long fingernails were caked with old blood. His shirt was half torn open, and he leaped onto my back. I struggled, swiping my paws awkwardly, roaring and snapping my jaws, but his amazingly strong hands pushed me down, one of his thin knees digging into my spine. The panther shook with rage, and the human side of me screamed with horror as fingernails bit into my shoulders.

Then the weight was gone. I was on my feet in a second, shaking my fur and looking into the calm, eerily serene face of Laylian. The vampire that had just moments ago been on my back leaped toward him, seeming to hang suspended in the air for a long moment. Laylian stepped easily out of the way and the vampire rolled into the spot where he'd been just moments ago, spinning on his heel, half hanging shirt bursting its final button and pooling around his feet.

Laylian pulled long, thin blade from a sheath on his back, and with one swift swing the rogue vampire's head was rolling to bump against my front paw. Black blood spurted from the stump that used to be a neck for a moment, then the thin body of the old man possessing the strength of ten young ones fell to its knees. It jerked spasmodically then fell lifeless to the ground, turning to dust. Laylian winked and disappeared from view.

176

Where the hell was Trace?

I got my answer in the form of a howl. I turned, tail swishing nervously. Three vampires were circling Trace. He snarled, his big, white head dipped low, and backed up a few inches. By the shifting of his human-green eyes I could see that he was trying to decide which of the vampires to attack first. He didn't have to choose.

A bulky, short, pale brunet male in a black wife-beater ran forward. Trace ran, then soared, meeting the vampire in mid-air. His lips pulled back from his teeth and he caught the vampire on one muscled shoulder. The vampire turned to dust and Trace shook his head to loosen a piece of black fabric that had caught in his teeth.

I ran, my steps light and my ears flat, pebbles flying in all directions as my wide paws slapped the earth. My mouth watered as I zeroed in on my target—a tall, thin female with long silky red hair. She wore leather, and appeared to be much more conscious of simple hygiene and fashion than the other rogues. She was hunkered low, preparing to jump on Trace's back as he and another ragged-looking male vampire circled each other.

Then she tensed, seeing my speedy approach. She whirled and her long red hair shimmered in the moonlight. A lovely, lightly freckled peaches-and-cream face stared wide-eyed and furious. I almost hesitated. I almost stopped to appreciate the flawless beauty, but the panther wanted her blood.

Her red eyes blazed with hatred, her pretty full mouth turned white as it stretched to expose her fangs and she ran, long nails curled in front of her, mouth open and ready to rip a chunk out of my silky black hide. My panther roared, darted to the side at the moment we were about to collide and caught her on the hip, incisors sinking easily into the gentle swell of her tender flesh.

Bitter-tasting liquid filled my mouth for maybe half a second, then turned to ashes on my tongue. She literally made a *poof* sound as she exploded into nothing. Ashes fell into my eyes and covered my fur. I caught a glimpse of Trace extinguishing the tall vampire with a bite on the vampire's outstretched arm as he punched, barely missing Trace's snout.

Battle cries carried all around, and the cheetah I'd seen earlier ran by, its body like a yellow bullet in the night as it leaped onto the back of a muscular black vampire in a black polo shirt.

Behind me two vampires rolled on the ground. I recognized the female from our group. A short stocky Asian man in tall black boots pressed the length of a metal baseball bat to her throat. She wheezed, grasping for the dagger on her thigh that was partially hanging from its sheath. Her eyes changed from a bright, blazing red to a dull pink as her movements grew slower. Her face was turning a mottled red, and I faintly wondered if vampires could suffocate. But the panther had no desire to reflect on questions and was running toward the struggle, a mixture of hissing vampire battle cries and animal growling filling my ears from the blurring-fast war around me.

But as I approached, the female's hand wrapped around the blue hilt of her dagger and her lips pulled back with effort as she stabbed it into the neck of the Asian vampire straddling her. His hands left the bat and clawed at her arm as she savagely sawed at his throat, black, smoking blood dripping onto her face and sizzling against her flesh. I skidded to a halt beside them, opening my mouth wide and biting down on the back of his skull. As soon as my teeth met bone he turned to ash that rained onto her shoulders. She spat, pushed herself weakly into a sitting position and wiped at the acidic blood covering her cheeks. She nodded her thanks, then was running off into the mass of twisting and clashing bodies. Somewhere from inside the fight, a gunshot sounded, causing me to instinctively hunker down.

I smelled Trace before I saw him, a mixture of spice and the musky, heady scent of wolf. The battle was growing quieter, and I was ready to spring into the belly of it when they came.

I was under the delusion that we were winning. I was almost gloating with my simple kills. I should have known that it would never be that simple, but I couldn't sense the new arrivals with so much stimulation around me and the hunger for more kills thrumming in my veins.

The first attackers had been but a distraction.

A black, blurring wave of bodies crested the hill and I occasionally caught a glimpse of a snarling face or the flash of a crude weapon. There were way more than I'd thought, and with a quick estimate, I guessed that there were at least a hundred rogue vampires barreling our way, maybe more. The battle at my side went oddly silent and I heard Laylian shouting something that sounded like an order to retreat. Trace was tense beside me, staring at the approaching army with his ears perked, tail low. He met my eyes, nudged me with his snout, and stomped his great white paws.

"Run!" I heard him in my head as clearly as if he'd spoken it, and the shock of his telepathic order made me take a step back, confused and shaken. He pushed me harder with his snout, painfully ramming it into the softness of my side, and snapped at the air. Then he shifted again, turning into an animal I'd never seen in person—a Bald eagle. He took to the air in a moment, flying toward our group. My human fear fought for control and the panther physically jerked with annoyance. The panther wanted blood, it wanted to rage, and it wanted to tear the approaching vampires' throats out one by one. I was at war with myself, torn between wanting to stay and fight—even if it meant certain death—and longing to turn tail and run.

Then Laylian was at my side, slapping me smartly on my flank and shouting for me to run, to hide, to get as far away as I could and keep running until I made it back to civilization. I had a sudden visual of Oz and Aunt Mag sitting at the kitchen table of the cabin, waiting for my return. I thought of Mom, her head swollen with the terrible, vile thing growing inside, then leaping toward me after I'd agreed to let Laylian transform her into a blood-drinking monster, her face contorted with rage and hunger. I felt human terror creeping, swelling, and finally overriding my bloodlust. Laylian had disappeared, meeting one of the first vampires to reach the group, sinking his long, curled fingernails into its eyes. The male vampire flew backward, clawing at his face, hissing as black blood rolled down his cheeks. The group looked so very small when compared to the approaching army, having not even finished off the first group of rogues.

But something was wrong. My energy was slowly ebbing away. It was as if I'd sprung a power leak. I had the disturbing sensation of bugs skittering over my body, of something prodding me from the inside out, and I shook my fur, dancing backward and scanning the area around me for my tormentor. A weird smell assaulted my nose. I couldn't place it, but I'd smelled something similar before. It was vampire, yes, but it was something else too. Something even more vile.

Then I was naked. A straggler enemy stumbled into my line of vision, leftover from the first wave, and he hissed, one of his hands missing and spurting blood onto his startlingly white sneakers. I called for the panther, wishing like hell I'd learned to control my shift better before being forced to take the risk I'd taken tonight, but it stalked helplessly inside as my fear took over.

I shrieked, not giving a damn that I was as naked as the day I was born, and turned to run.

Trace. Trace. His name whispered with every thud of my heart. What if he didn't make it? What if they were unable to retreat? What if they stayed and fought until each of them were dead and left me alone to face them all by myself? The rogue vampires' numbers were too great, and even with shifters in the group there wouldn't be enough of them to go around to help.

They'd trusted me to lead them here. They'd trusted me to know the vampires' location, and I'd unintentionally screwed everything up by alerting their leader. And even if the beings in my group were all monsters in their own way, I couldn't stand to fathom them all meeting their ends because of me.

I fled, tears popping into the corners of my eyes, my nude body breaking into a sweat and my feet screaming with pain as I ran over sharp pebbles on the dirt path that led steeply down toward the mine. I didn't have a clue where I was going and I gasped, arms pumping, willing my panther to come to the surface. It wasn't working.

Something thin and rough rubbed my wrist, and I wondered how the bracelet had survived the shift. Magic, I supposed.

The bracelet!

What had Pearl said? The feather of a hawk, the fur of a bear…the? I couldn't remember. But if I could just focus… if I could just calm myself long enough, I could possibly fly my way back to the cabin.

I summoned the last of what I now knew was my magic — that spark I felt tingling my skin, the energy that was somehow connected to the earth, the trees, to everything. I focused on a hawk. I pictured it gliding effortlessly through the air, its brown, feathered head being ruffled by the wind, its wings spread wide.

Then I was flopping to the ground in an awkward heap, feathers puffing around me. I panicked, flapping my wings frantically, tiny, taloned feet biting into the dirt. This body didn't feel like the comfortable skin of my panther. It felt weird, unnatural. The shift to panther was seamless, like stepping into the most comfortable pair of slippers, but the hawk was gangly and alien, like a borrowed skin, not connected to my soul like my true form. Then I was myself again, finding myself face down in the dirt, a strange tug pulling at my navel, the sixth sense that all human's possess screaming that something was close, that something was chasing me.

I groaned, stumbling to my feet and jogging naked down

the sloping hill that was tattooed with tire tracks from ATVs. I tried to pace myself lest I build up too much momentum and tumble to the bottom, but every nerve screamed at me to *hurry the hell up, hurry the hell up. You're going to die. Run faster, idiot. Run faster.*

Why couldn't I give my panther control?

Then I smelled it—death and magic that was so foul it couldn't have been anything but evil. Then a sensation crashed into me, something I'd felt back on the riding trail turned battlefield. The panther yawned, shook its head somewhere down in the pits of my inner darkness, and ignored my pleas for help. My body suddenly felt loose, drugged, and I stumbled as I reached the bottom of the hill. A rocky, steep hillside rose maybe fifty feet in front of me, and at its base a small, dark hole with supporting timbers around its edges appeared.

The deep mine. It was my only hope, and at the moment the rogue vampires were behind me, possibly exterminating the group of vampires and shifters that had trusted me to make sure I was leading them into a successful ambush.

The wind suddenly felt chilly on my exposed skin, and my hair had tangled around my chin like a veil. I brushed it away, pulling the wayward tangles free and flinging them over my bare shoulder.

Maybe it was magic, maybe it was just intuition, but I knew that something was coming and if I didn't move fast, I would end up being a side dish. I could see much better than I used to. I'd had perfect vision all of my life, but now it was wonderful, even in weak moonlight, but the prospect of being in the dark tunnel that was under thousands of pounds of dirt just one wrong vibration away from burying me made me shiver.

I had to hide. A huge part of me wanted to go back and assure myself that Trace was alive. I didn't really know why it was so important to me that he survived. I'd known him a whole half a week, and it wasn't as if I had feelings for him. Right?

But something was growing, there was no way to deny it. I felt drawn to him in a way that was far more complicated than a confused crush. I felt…I felt like I was almost meant to know him, like he was some important part of my destiny.

But the other part of me knew that Trace and the mixed group of vampires and shifters were more experienced, the majority being professionally trained in combat, and in my current soft, useless state I would only be a liability. Something had zapped my magic, something didn't want me to shift, and if I dared go back to stupidly play the hero I would be running into certain death.

I took a deep, shaky breath, and plunged into the mine.

I stayed in the center of the track, feeling my way with the damp, rocky walls of the tunnel. I bumped into something large. It rattled and rolled a little down the track, making a grinding, rumbling noise. A cart—an old one from the rusty, corroded feel of it. The way the workers rode to their destination at the beginning of their shifts and traveled out at the end of it.

I'd thought that I'd have the advantage with me improved vision, but the deeper I walked the darker it became. Pretty soon I was feeling my way, occasionally scaring the living shit out of myself when my shuffling feet sent a rock or an old soda can bouncing, echoing in the tunnel. I assumed the old workers had tossed the trash out on their rides to and fro, or someone had been partying by lantern light. Once or twice something wiggled under my palm as I felt my way through and I had to swallow a scream. I was feeling weaker by the second, and all too humanly exhausted. Was it just the past few days catching up with me? I felt the insect skittering sensation over my skin again and was overwhelmed by a strange sense of loss. I couldn't help it, I cried out, coming to a stop and wiping at my eyes.

Occasionally I'd smack roughly into what felt like a tree trunk. I didn't know much about mines, but I knew there were timbers leading up to the beams meant to support the earth above to keep the roof from collapsing

I'd never felt so defenseless in my entire life.

Pretty soon my legs were dragging, and I instinctively knew that the warm liquid I felt on the pads of my feet was my own blood. I stumbled, hugging myself for warmth as the air grew cooler, nearly frigid, and my teeth chattered uncontrollably.

I almost thought it a trick of my imagination when I saw a soft glow of light just around a long, snaking curve on the track. My heart thumped like a jackhammer in my chest and adrenaline shot through my numb, naked legs. I ran toward the light, tears streaming down my cheeks, sobbing my thanks to God. It was a lantern hanging from a large spike that had been pounded into the rocky wall on the right side of the tunnel. I made it to the lantern, knowing that I should find a better hiding place, but was too exhausted to go any farther.

The soft light chased away a few shadows, and that was good enough for me.

I'd never heard such perfect silence. I sat exposed beneath the lamp, my bare legs hugged to my chest, and knew that I'd sell my soul for a robe if given the chance. Occasionally water would drip from somewhere farther down the tunnel, the only interruption, the only audible thing that convinced me I was still alive.

How long had I been cowering in the tunnel? How many minutes, or hours had passed since I'd listened to Trace for once and hauled ass as far away as I could from the danger? Had anyone survived? Would the vampires be free to wipe out the town? I guessed that even if there were only a hundred of them, that was more than enough to do the job. I'd seen things during that battle that hinted at just how indestructible they were. From what I'd witnessed, the only quick, sure way to kill a vampire was to remove the head, and to a bunch of rural citizens who were more fond of pistols than of swords, that wouldn't be an easy task.

Only my kind was capable of turning the vampires into dust with a quick bite or scratch. We were the ultimate weapon against evil—and here I was, hiding in a cave, unable to even touch the power I had fought so hard against before.

What had changed?

Amazingly, twice I nodded off only to jerk myself awake and bang my head on a rock behind me. Would Trace find me?

I wanted Oz. I wanted my mom back the way she once was, before she'd gotten sick. I wanted Aunt Mag and her makeshift-mommy attitude, and I realized with more than a little surprise that I wanted Trace just as badly.

Even if he was a prideful, cocky punk hell-bent on digging as far under my skin as possible, he was a solid presence that made me feel safe. Something told me with a certainty that he would do whatever it took to keep me safe, even if he hated me. Was it my rare talents that made him so concerned over my safety, or something more? He hovered protectively any time he was around me, almost as if I might vanish if he didn't keep me directly within his view. What did it mean?

I blew into my cupped hands, trying to melt off some of the numbness, and seriously considered stretching out on the filthy, coal-blackened surface beside the rusty track. My shadow looked huge on the opposite wall, and I was so confused that I startled myself by moving a few times, causing my shadow to move with me. I laughed softly to myself, finding morbid amusement when I looked at the situation a certain way.

I was butt naked in an abandoned coal mine, jumping at my own shadow and wishing I could turn into a giant cat. I was sort of surprised to find that I didn't crave a joint. Instead I craved my magic. I craved the shift, but it was slowly inching far away from me at such a steady rate that I wondered if it was leaving me forever.

"Here, kitty, kitty." The voice was musical, accented with French, and reminded me of a clear, bubbling stream.

My head whipped around and the rocks on my bare

back bit in painfully as I cowered against the wall, my feet pressed against the side of the track in front of me. I pushed harder at the dirt, wishing it could swallow me up, and I covered my mouth with my hand to keep from screaming. I should have been up and running. But I felt so human, so frail, so weak, and I wouldn't make it far. I tried to urge myself up anyway, but my butt didn't make it an inch off the ground before it was plopping back onto small, jagged pieces of rock and bits of coal.

He'd been waiting for me.

Something horrible twisted in my gut, nipping and pinching, exploring my fears, and I felt the last of my strength drain away. It was him. The albino. *And he's somehow taking my strength. He's taking it, and keeping it for his own. He's more than I thought, so much more than I thought.*

My head lolled back and I used what little strength I had to keep my eye on the corner where the glow of the lamp began to die.

A tall, lean form stepped into view. Long white hair was tied back and a sleek ponytail that lay over one shoulder. He wore black slacks, and even though it was summer and hot as blazes outside, a long-sleeved, black wool turtleneck. Black, well-polished loafers kicked at a small piece of coal lying on the track, and he smiled in what almost looked like welcome, the white, thick scar running from his ear to the corner of his mouth obvious even in the sparse light. He wrinkled his long nose and his lips quirked at the corner.

"You're just as lovely as I imagined, disgustingly filthy but lovely, nonetheless. And look at you…not a stitch of clothing. I see you've gone through great lengths to make this as simple as possible for me."

The panther jerked weakly, struggling to wake, only to fall, exhausted, back into hiding. I felt strangely abandoned and annoyed. A few days earlier I would have rejoiced at the panther's departure, but now I would have given anything to have fur instead of the delicate, bare white skin I trembled violently in.

"You thought your witchery was enough? You thought it would give your group the advantage? Hmmm? You are not the only one educated in the arts. You're not the only hybrid. I was born both warlock and vampire. My mother was a witch, my father a vampire born pure of blood. The result of such a match was a powerful being, both natural warlock and perfect vampire. Your father must have been very strong, no? You are talented, but you reek of inexperience."

I wondered if my father had been such a hybrid. Had his mother been a warlock? His father a shifter? Vice versa? I really didn't care, and I'd never really know, because my struggle would end tonight. I'd die in a dark tunnel far back in the earth at the hands of a monster. I'd grown into my magic, only to have it stamped out before I'd even explored it. I'd made my mother into a monster, dragged my best friend into a world he didn't belong in, and had led a bunch of the good guys into a one-sided battle tonight.

"You tried to get into my head, no? My people have been watching you since you gathered in front of that shack the old bitch calls home. Her magic is strong, but her bindings are not enough to restrain a revolutionary such as myself. We are the alpha species, we are at the top of the food chain, yet Laylian forces us to stand in line for sustenance as if we were homeless beggars in a soup kitchen. It is our nature to hunt, yet we are forbidden. He fears that we will grow to bold and overthrow him, but some of us recognize him as weak. He clings to old-fashioned ways, human ways. I am changing that. The resistance is not only here, we are everywhere. The head counsel is weakening and losing its hold. I want to see submission in the eyes of my prey, not a drugged woman who pulls her hair back and reveals a neck defiled with many bites from many others."

He spat, and his face contorted as he flipped his long platinum hair away from his brow. He took a deep breath, and when he met my eyes again, I knew that I'd reached my end.

187

I wished he'd get it over with. I hoped it would be quick. I hoped it wouldn't hurt, that he wouldn't let me suffer, that it would be pleasant like the first vampire bite I'd gotten. The scar, which had been deep puncture wounds just days before, throbbed as if sensing another set of fangs nearby. He smiled into my face, gently brushing his long, bejeweled fingers through my wild, tangled hair.

Brass laughed. "Little shifter. How curious I am about your taste. Will you be sweet like honey? Will you be bitter with white magic? Will it be as enjoyable without the power I have drained of you? I cannot use your power to shift as you do, but I feel so very strong with its energy. I haven't felt quite so excited in some time. You have restored my passion, and for that I will make your death a pleasant one. But I must know, do you crave me the way that I crave you?"

He kissed my cheek. His lips were so cold I expected them to stick to my skin, frozen. I wanted to see my mom before I died, even if she wasn't the woman I had known and loved my entire life. Would she cry for me and grieve? Or would she just be jealous that she hadn't been the one to drain me?

His eyes raked over my body and he pulled my face to his, kissing me roughly, bruising my immobile lips. I'd never wanted clothes so badly in my entire life. Dying would suck, yes, but I would have much rather died with my lady bits covered. Death has a way of making anyone look vulnerable, and I didn't want to look any more pathetic than necessary when, and if, anyone found me.

I could feel the fangs slide into the opposite side of my throat from where the first vampire had bitten me. The pain was sharp, exquisite, and though I told myself I wouldn't give him the satisfaction, I couldn't keep myself from crying out. My fingers curled to weak fists, my legs kicked feebly and I felt my eyes rolling back into my head.

Then his fangs were ripped away, slicing the meat of my throat with an awful wet noise. My eyes swam back into focus and I saw Trace in his wolf form. His giant white

188

head whipped back and forth, tearing at the flesh of Brass' shoulders as he pinned him with his considerable bulk to the center of the tracks.

Something small and gray shot by — a coyote from the looks of it — and joined him in his assault. I spotted Michelle running close behind, glossy dark hair carrying like strands of silk behind her. I wondered why Brass wasn't exploding into ashes like the other vampires, and figured that he was more powerful than any of us had imagined. He clawed and bucked wildly, and I saw a red stain spread on Trace's side. Michelle halted in front of me, looked at the scuffle on the ground, and charged me.

Some of the feeling had returned to my fingers in the last few moments. It was like the distraction of Trace's attack and the coyote shifter had momentarily paused the leeching of power Brass had been using to render me helpless. Both sides of my personality froze, confused, as Michelle soared through the air. I expected to have the oxygen I was struggling to breathe in knocked out of me, but instead she lifted me up with her thin tan arms, threw me over her delicate-looking shoulder, and ran in the opposite direction of the scuffle so fast that I wasn't sure if we were running or flying. Apparently vampires were fast, superman fast, and I felt something almost like admiration as she blurred through the dark tunnel, my weight on her shoulder not fazing her in the least. In no time we were at the entrance and she tossed me unceremoniously to the dusty earth in a heap.

"You stupid little bitch! Why does he want to protect you so badly? Who cares if you're a tracker? Who cares what you can turn into? Look at where your talent has gotten us! We've lost ten vampires tonight, and two of your shifters, and do you know what Trace was concerned about? Not his own, not himself, but *you*."

My voice was a croak, thick with snot and hoarse from breathing in the cold tunnel air.

"He's his own person. I didn't ask him to protect me."

189

Her beautiful face contorted with rage. "He told me to get you out of the mine. He said, '*Even if I am dying, don't help, just get her to safety'*. I should have left you there! I should have collapsed the entrance and buried you there before he went inside. A little piece of advice? Stay away from him, because I will not follow orders for your sake again. He's *mine*. You are but a fascination. You're new, I understand that, a novelty, but soon that will fade. He warms my bed, not yours."

I knew two things then. One — she loved Trace. Two — she wanted me dead, and if given the opportunity she would snap my neck like a twig.

But I ignored her. I pushed myself into a sitting position with effort. Something soft smacked against the side of my face and I picked up the jacket Michelle had had tied around her waist.

"Put that on. You look like a filthy animal. No one wants to see your white ass."

My neck ached where I'd been bitten and I gingerly reached up to touch the open wound on my neck. The skin felt feverish and I knew that soon I'd need Pearl's doctoring. I winced, hoping that it wouldn't be as terrible as the last time I'd been gnawed on I seemed to be handling this bite better, what with being conscious and all, so maybe I'd built up some weird tolerance? I didn't know.

I flipped Michelle off and held the fabric against my chest, keeping my eyes on the entrance of the tunnel. I heard a soft rustle and Laylian came into view. He said nothing, but put his cold hand on my shoulder. I managed not to shiver in disgust. I knew what he was doing, he was trying to comfort me. Somehow he knew that I blamed myself, and something in my eyes as I looked up into his face must have conveyed just how sorry I was.

"No sign?" he asked Michelle.

"No. Brass is powerful. He was rumored to dabble in the dark arts. After what I saw, I have no doubt it's true. He was holding on against a bite from two shifters at once."

Laylian sighed.

There were others behind us and Laylian ordered them inside the cave. Five vampires and one shifter instantly obeyed, and entered the mine without looking back or hesitating.

Tears were prickling my eyes and my vision blurred as they threatened to spill onto my cheeks. If I could have stood, I would have gone stumbling back into the darkness. They would have had to restrain me. Even though I barely knew him, the thought of losing Trace so soon filled me with an emptiness that bordered on panic. I didn't know what the feelings meant, and I didn't care. I just wanted him alive. I needed him to walk out. I craved for him to terrorize me and insult me and hover over me like I was too stupid to function alone. I didn't care about his motivation. I didn't care if he even liked me, he just needed to be within reaching distance.

We waited for another twenty minutes, and I dipped my head, knowing that it was all my fault. Knowing that two more people had died because I'd accidentally tipped the rogue vampires off. I wondered who the coyote was who had helped Trace double-team Brass. Eventually someone passed me a shiny black leather trench coat, and I tossed Michelle's thin jacket in her direction without looking. I heard her mumble something that sounded like bitch, but I didn't care. The coat warmed my skin, but I trembled as if it were a sheet of ice. Each second felt like an hour, and my hope that Trace had survived Brass was ebbing quickly away. It seemed that everyone I cared about was dying in one way or another, and as a warm breeze cooled the sweat on my forehead, I couldn't help but wonder who would be next.

Aunt Mag? Oz? Me?

Laylian patted my shoulder awkwardly and Michelle was deathly silent. I didn't look at her, though, because I knew I'd see blame there, and something even more unsettling. Disgust.

"I didn't know. I think...I think that he knew all along somehow. I think that he's been watching me. This was his ambush from the beginning."

Laylian said nothing but I felt his hand tense so briefly that I could tell it was accidental. I felt warmth spreading through my shoulder...comfort, and under less frightening circumstances I would have leaned into his touch, maybe even asked for a back rub. He was using vampire magic of some kind, not as powerful as Pearl's but strong, nonetheless. The feeling he emitted was enough to still the panic attack I felt getting closer with each passing moment, and I was thankful.

The remaining shifters and vampires were crowded behind us. I could hear their voices, soft, conversational, as if they were at a funeral. I scrubbed at my dirty cheeks with the back of one hand. I just wanted to go home. I wanted my bed. I wanted everything to go back to the way it was before Mom got sick. When things were sane, and problems didn't involve evil vampires and shapeshifting. When I was waiting for death and hopeless. Although awful, it had been better that way. Better than feeling hope and having it dashed over and over again.

Then I heard a groan.

I tensed, quirking my head to listen with my new, sensitive hearing. I heard it again. Definitely a groan. Trace hopped into view, followed by an unharmed-looking coyote with black blood staining its snout. Trace had on jeans he hadn't been wearing earlier, and I wondered how he'd gotten them considering the shift didn't agree with clothing too well. My question was answered as a very prim-looking male vampire walked out behind him, smiley face boxers yellow and painfully loud in the darkness. He looked as if he'd just swallowed something sour, and I wondered dimly if it was possible for a vampire to blush.

"Trace!" Michelle shrieked happily and ran toward him, arms outstretched. But Trace dodged her just before she wrapped her arms around him. His vivid green eyes were boring into mine, his black hair sticking to his forehead with sweat. His side was bleeding a little, and blood had soaked through his borrowed blue jeans, but as he got closer I could see that the wound on his side was already healing. He picked up the pace, wincing with every step, and my heart jumped into my throat.

I'd never been so relieved in my entire life.

Trace broke into an awkward run, and when he reached me, let himself fall with to his knees in front of me, his face inches from mine. He looked as relieved as I felt as he placed a hand on each side of my face, his eyes roaming over my body, taking in the trench coat that gaped brazenly open in front despite my efforts to hold it closed and preserve whatever dignity I had left among the random creatures lurking about.

Then he was crushing me against him, releasing a long breath that sounded as if he'd been holding it for a very long time. I began to cry, not caring if the trench coat slipped or who was watching. I'd never felt anything more natural than the skin-to-skin contact we made as I snaked my arms around his neck.

"You're alive. You saved me," I mumbled against his hair, the silky midnight strands clinging to my face. I tasted the salt of his sweat and breathed in the comforting, cinnamon-spicy smell of him.

It was shocking, and the most unexpected thing on the planet when he pulled away just far enough to tip my face up to his, his rough fingers gentle under my chin. His kiss was featherlight, warm, and a balm to the mental and physical pain I'd been drowning in all night. He kissed both of my cheeks and pressed his forehead to mine. And I didn't protest. Not even once.

"There's going to be more, Wren, but I'm going to keep you safe. I swear it."

I nodded, not wanting to think about the future. The only thing I wanted was to stay in his arms and listen to him speak. His promise to keep me safe had given me more joy and comfort than I'd ever known.

"Where will I go?" I asked, knowing that my home was no longer a haven. Knowing that if I stayed with Aunt Mag, she would die.

"I have somewhere in mind. We'll talk about it later, okay? I was scared, Wren. I really believed we'd be too late."

"It's okay," I said, sounding small and uncertain. I knew he wasn't comfortable admitting weakness, and the newness of all the emotions that roiled through me made my head spin.

I hugged him close.

I hadn't seen any of the vampires go back into the mine, but they must have, because a dark-skinned man with long glossy black hair emerged carrying the tiny, curled body of the red-haired woman.

I gasped, realizing that in all my terror, I hadn't thought about her. It made me feel shitty and selfish. Her eyes were closed but I could tell by the careful way the dark-skinned vampire carried her that she was alive. How would this be explained to her if she woke up? I decided not to think about it too hard, although it sounded like a job for Pearl and her mind-fucks.

I thought of Oz and a jolt of guilt made me physically jerk. I felt Trace stiffen but I snuggled closer. He relaxed again, breathing against my tangled hair. Why did I feel like I was doing something wrong, as if I were betraying Oz in some way? I didn't want to think about that. Trace had come into my life like a whirlwind. From the moment I'd met him, all had been chaos, but the unexplainable bond and the overwhelming desire to touch him and taste him as he held me tightly in his arms both terrified and thrilled me. Something strange was happening. I suddenly knew, without a doubt, that we were meant for each other. He was my mate, a crucial piece of my future.

Then I understood the protectiveness he'd been displaying all along. He'd been feeling this for longer than I had. He too knew without a doubt that our souls were somehow entwined, that we were somehow wrapped in each other's destinies. That we were each a missing half meant to help make the other whole. The Wren who had stumbled aimlessly through life for the past three months fell away, replaced with a girl who had begun to feel something she'd almost completely lost — hope.

Over his shoulder, at the entrance of the cave, my sight zoomed in unwillingly on Michelle's face. The zoom-vision still came without warning, and I really had no idea how to control it. I hoped I'd live to learn.

My eyes focused on the single, solitary tear as it ran down her cinnamon cheek.

"It's okay," I told him again, almost as if I believed it.

About the Author

Selina Rose Fugate

Selina lives in the gorgeous mountains of Perry County, Kentucky with her two children and a devious cat. When she's not outside playing with her kiddos, or looking for fairies under flower petals, she's dreaming up tales that will hopefully make those that read them smile.

You can take a look at Selina's Website and follow her on Facebook and Twitter.

Selina Rose Fugate loves to hear from readers. You can find contact information, website details and an author profile page at https://www.finch-books.com/